Open Conspiracy

Open Conspiracy

Graham Porter

ROBERT HALE · LONDON

© Graham Porter 1998
First published in Great Britain 1998

ISBN 0 7090 6168 4

Robert Hale Limited
Clerkenwell House
Clerkenwell Green
London EC1R 0HT

The right of Graham Porter to be identified as
author of this work has been asserted by him
in accordance with the Copyright, Designs and
Patents Act 1988.

2 4 6 8 10 9 7 5 3 1

Photoset in North Wales by
Derek Doyle & Associates, Mold, Flintshire.
Printed in Great Britain by
St Edmundsbury Press, Bury St Edmunds, Suffolk.
Bound by WBC Book Manufacturers Limited, Bridgend.

1

Ah, the Masters! How thoughtful and perceptive of them to have invited him to compete! So here he was at last, striding up the eighteenth fairway, no longer a middle-aged businessman with a high handicap but a veritable Adonis of a man — flat bellied and steely nerved — tipping his winning cap to thunderous cheering as the crowd rose to its feet, welcoming their surprising new golfing hero.

Soon he would don the green jacket as had Nicklaus and Palmer and Watson. Yes, and as Faldo and Tiger Woods! But at this moment, as he stepped on to the final green, he smiled with embarrassment as several young women bolted from the traditionally decorous crowd to race his way, causing the marshals an unprecedented problem. He tried not to stare in awed anticipation as a particularly coltish blonde broke free from a security guard and raced towards him, closer and closer, her breasts gyrating like two volleyballs gone berserk.

'Henry! ... Are you all right?'

He opened his eyes to the darkness of the bedroom, reality slowly swimming into focus. The voice of his wife seemed fraught with concern. 'You woke me with your sudden panting, Henry. Were you having a nightmare?'

'Well ... uh ... not exactly.'

'You were dreaming about golf, weren't you? What happened? Did you drive your cart into that pond again?'

He rolled on to his back, deeming it best not to answer.

'Honestly, Henry, that silly game is becoming more of an obsession with you all the time ... I mean, *honestly*!' With that she sank down on to her pillow and plunged back into a sea of sleep.

Like a mackerel awash on the sand, Henry Summerfill flopped onto his back, his eyes now refusing to close. Even in the midnight darkness he could detect the gash mark that he had placed on the ceiling last January while taking too enthusiastic a practice swing with his five-iron. At the time he had tried to convince Martha that it had simply been a freakish household accident. Unfortunately his wife had been quick to point out that only a month earlier he had also freakishly whacked out a sizeable divot from the living-room carpet. Now, as she slept beside him, he tried to force those episodes from his mind in the same manner as he attempted to forget that despite years of caring and striving and study, his golfing handicap remained in the upper teens. His only consolation had been that there was always tomorrow. But he had long since kissed his fortieth birthday goodbye, and his golfing tomorrows were growing dishearteningly fewer now. His concept of a real man was a guy who pounded out long drives and rammed home clutch-putts, not some staid business-suited accountant like himself whose crunching of fiscal numbers was frequently distracted by fantasy-inducing office-girls who kept flaunting their round little bottoms only at younger men with lower handicaps.

Henry ran a hand through his thinning hair and forced his eyes shut. Despite his resolve to count sheep he found himself counting golf strokes instead. As he mentally replayed each shot of his afternoon's round he permitted himself the benefit of the doubt on some of the bad breaks he had fallen heir to during the reality of his game. Now with nerves of steel he sank the three short putts he had missed earlier and he straightened out the tee shot he had sliced out of bounds. When he subtracted those strokes from his posted score of ninety-two he discovered that for all practical purposes he had shot a respectable eighty-seven.

Or might he not have scored better still! There was no denying he had been victimized by other quirks of fate as well. A perfect pitch shot to the ninth green had taken an astounding hop into a bunker, costing him a triple bogey. His drive on the twelfth had taken cover beneath the only bramble-bush on the entire course. And on the seventeenth, a caddie had sneezed at the top of his backswing, all but making him miss the ball completely. Henry stared wide-eyed into the darkness as he subtracted those minor but well-deserved deductions from his hypothetical eighty-seven. When he arrived at the amazing figure of seventy-nine his body seemed to float towards the gash-marked ceiling.

Why was it, he wondered, that non-golfers could in no way comprehend how the game could take hold of a person so completely. On various occasions he had been tempted to explain the psychology of it to Martha, but he suspected it would end up in one of those husband-wife debates which he never won. Yet, some day he should give it a try . . . . *You see, dear,* he would begin, *golf isn't like tennis or squash or any of those other foolish slam-bang sports. When those games are over you're left with nothing more than a vague impression of having played poorly or well. But with golf – ah, that's different! Each swing you take sticks in your memory. And you know that the course is just lying in wait to test you again. It's almost like the Devil himself is after you!*

But Henry, she would interrupt, *that's my whole point. The*

7

fact that it leads only to frustration and anguish just doesn't make sense. Why can't you simply treat it as a pleasurable pastime?

Golf is more than a pastime, Martha. It's even more than a sport. It's the last remaining bastion of pure individualism – the only means left for a man to prove himself solely on his own capabilities.

I thought the business world was man's proving ground?

Henry would shoot down that argument as well . . . . *I'm going to ask you to open your mind, dear – to think in broad philosophic terms, OK? In business it's no longer possible to measure one's personal contribution. It gets lost in a maze of economic influences and conferences and lawyers and government restrictions* . . . . He would then lower the speed and pitch of his voice so that she might imagine his next words were being uttered by Socrates himself. *Golf is but a microcosm of the world as it was meant to be before modern society screwed it up – a journey through life, if you will, in which a man can still measure the attainments of his own mind and muscle and nerve – a world of fears and frustrations, yes, but also a world filled with eternal hope and glorious dreams – dreams that just might, some day, come true* . . . .

Under such an eloquent barrage of logic Martha surely would capitulate, perhaps even urging him to resign from the accountancy firm of Brenham, Scofield and Meade to devote the rest of his life to the noble pursuit of golf.

Having thus successfully concluded his make-believe marital dialogue, Henry found himself too charged up to lie still. Ever so cautiously, so as not to alert Martha or his twelve-year-old daughter in the next room, he slithered from bed, placed his glasses on the bridge of his nose and reached for an imaginary driver. He then swept his body through such a powerful and smooth swing that, had the situation been born in reality, the ball would surely have zoomed into orbit. In the dim, utter stillness of the bedroom, Henry Summerfill (with just a hint of exertion) threw out his chest and pulled in his stomach and exuded more confidence than ever before in his life.

Confidence! Ah, so that was the key! How incredible to realize that in all these years while he had been gorging his mind with mechanical do's and don'ts, it had instead been fear alone that had robbed him of the calibre of golf he knew to be his natural destiny. Had Henry's eyes not already grown bloodshot from lack of sleep they would have twinkled as brightly as the April stars outside his window. Alex Wulf was about to have his come-uppance. Season after season, Henry's arch rival had beaten on him like a drum, shattering his pride and depleting his wallet. In the night's shadows, Henry gave birth to a wicked chuckle. Tomorrow when they met as opponents in the Club's team handicap tournament perhaps he would suggest to Alex that they should double their usual bet.

2

A few precious hours beyond Henry Summerfill's nocturnal land of illusion lay the uncompromising world of reality. And nowhere was that world less prone to treat him with compassion than on the deceptively pastoral landscape of the Rolling Hills Country Club. Today, as if chastising him for his last night's impertinent dream, the first seventeen holes had all but shattered his nerves and broken his spirit. Only because of the steady play of his partner, Dwight Lyon, their first-round match in the team handicap tournament was not yet lost.

Now with driver in hand Henry stared down the eighteenth fairway from the tee. This was it – the match boiled down to this final hole. When he attempted a deep and calming breath, his respiratory tract responded with something akin to a death-rattle. At the moment neither war nor pestilence nor international economic disaster seemed quite so consequential as whether or not his next tee shot should prove successful.

'You can do it, Henry,' Dwight was saying. 'You're the only one with a handicap stroke here.'

When Henry rose from spearing his tee into the turf he was appalled at how the scene ahead was transforming itself before his bespectacled eyes. Even as he watched, the rough was growing taller and the fairway narrower, and, as if he were gazing through the wrong end of a telescope, the green itself, 345 yards away, was swiftly fleeing from sight over the distant horizon. If those factors were not discouraging enough, the dark entwining branches of the dogwood trees that lined the fairway – not yet in blossom on this mid-April day – seemed to be growing new tentacles, each reaching out in hopes of claiming his ball for its own. He would have felt more secure teeing off in the Vienna Woods.

Henry rubbed the clammy palm of his hand against his trouser leg and took his stance at the ball . . . . *Think smart, Henry,* he instructed himself. *You don't have to drive the ball a country mile. All you need are two decent, straight shots to nearly reach the green. Then it's simply a chip and a putt. That's all there is to it.*

But unfortunately, in the cold light of day, Henry Summerfill often found himself haunted by another interior voice – one that his rational nature had no dominion over at all. Now, at the worst possible moment that voice insisted on having its say . . . . *Jesus, Henry, stop fiddling around with your stinking stance and grip. Just rare back and let 'er fly. If you could out drive those other guys just once, think what that would do for your ego. After all, Greg Norman swings hard, doesn't he? And Tiger Woods? So why not Summerfill? . . . .* Henry wished the voice would go away and let him concentrate in peace. Right now he could use ten minutes of prayerful meditation and a good stiff drink. The facing wind that had died while the others in his foursome had teed off, had now sprung back to life with a vengeance, determined to rob every possible yard from his shot.

'My God, Henry,' cried his opponent, Alex Wulf. 'What are you waiting for, a gallery?'

With a half-sick grin, Henry addressed the ball. A moment later he found himself wildly adrift at the top of his backswing, the conscious level of his brain further adding to the confusion by trying to send a dozen simultaneous messages to his muscles. If there was any way in which he could have self-destructed, he would have done so without the slightest of qualms. As it was, he felt his body tip on to his toes as the clubhead met the ball, or, more precisely, met only a piece of it. He knew even before he observed its flight that it was identical to most of the drives he had hit all day – a weak, low shot that began its banana-shaped route towards the left before veering sharply to leap like a rabbit into the dogwoods bordering the right side of the fairway. Henry dropped his head, humiliated.

Seating himself in the moving golf cart beside his partner, Henry wondered whether by chance he had tumbled into the throes of that most illusive and insidious quirk of nature – the male counterpart of the menstrual cycle. True, the American Medical Association had yet to substantiate it as a bona fide malady, but he had once read there might well be such cyclical periods in sensitive men such as he when their emotional and physical competence just weren't up to snuff.

After chipping out from deep in the dogwoods, Henry watched the others in the foursome reach the green on their second shots, but none was close enough to the flag for a likely one-putt. It was then that he felt the burden of the match weigh solely on his shoulders. Unless he could get his ball into the hole in two more strokes, he and Dwight would lose the match. Or, more accurately, he, Henry Summerfill, would lose it for both of them.

For some time he plucked blades of grass from the emerald fairway, tossing them overhead to test the wind. In his distraught state, however, he kept neglecting to notice from which direction, if any, the breeze was blowing. Regardless of what he might have determined, he knew he was going to hit his three-wood anyway.

When he could procrastinate no longer he nervously took his stance. *All right, Henry,* he lectured himself, *easy does it. Eye on the ball, slow take away, finish high . . . .*

His resulting effort was deficient in only one respect – he began his beautiful high finish before reaching the bottom of his swing. Instead of the ball lifting itself skywards towards the flag, it skimmed along on a strafing mission not six feet above the fairway, veering in routine banana fashion towards the trap to the right of the green.

Henry's expression of horror reverted to one of ecstatic disbelief when his ball bounded against a trap rake, careered on to the putting surface and rolled to a stop not more than six feet from the pin. Dwight Lyon thumped him on the back with such vigour that Henry almost believed he had intentionally played the shot in just that manner. For the moment the world burst into beautiful radiance and he loved even Alex Wulf.

But when it came to his turn to putt the sun could not have snuffed itself out more quickly. He tried to keep his knees from quivering as he squatted behind his ball to line up his putt, then rose to step around behind the hole to line it up from that direction too. In neither case was he sure what he was supposed to be looking for.

Dwight Lyon, without so much as bothering to survey the contour, advised Henry that it was a straight putt with no break.

'Just don't leave it short.'

Henry Summerfill had not spent the winter practising his putting on the carpet for nothing. Night after night he had perfected his stroke until nineteen times out of twenty he could hit the leg of a chair from six feet away. And wasn't that the identical distance of this putt on the eighteenth green? As he placed his putter behind the ball he began checking himself out like the captain of a Boeing 767 . . . . Eye directly over the ball, *check* . . . . Gentle fingertip grip, *check* . . . . Putter blade square to hole, *check* . . . .

But in the midst of his final countdown that ugly inner voice rose up like ghost from Hell . . . . *You'll never make it Henry. This isn't like putting alone in your den or in one of your stupid day-dreams. This is for all the marbles. One tiny mistake in speed or direction and you've had it. See, already you're gripping your club as if trying to squeeze toothpaste from it. The truth is, old man, you're ill. Just feel the heaviness in your arms — the shallowness of your breathing! No way, Henry, no way . . . .*

Still the true voice of his manhood fought back . . . . *You can do it, Henry. Just get the ball to the hole. For God's sake, don't leave it short . . . . DON'T LEAVE IT SHORT . . . .*

3

'Henry, we're still planning on Europe in June, aren't we?'

Home from his golf game, Henry Summerfill stared past his wife out of the dining-room window where robins chirped and magnolias blossomed. But he no more heeded those delightful harbingers of spring than he heeded Martha's question. Only in the remotest corner of his consciousness did it register that she had made some reference to a charter flight to Paris sponsored by the garden clubs of the area. Months ago, when she had first suggested they should sign up, he had tried to forestall the issue by muttering non-committally. He should have known she would interpret his mutter as a go-ahead for reserving two seats on the plane for their first-ever visit to Europe.

Now she was talking again – something about the Wulfs having volunteered to look after Katie during their absence. Again, his mind, like a poorly tuned radio, failed to pick up his wife's frequency. All he heard was the name of the twelve-year-old daughter who at the moment, as so often, was engaged in some incomprehensible project in her scientific laboratory in the basement. Instead of acknowledging Martha's words with even a nod, Henry continued to finger his uneaten sandwich, his body inexplicably tired, a sodden lump still welling in his slightly rounded gut . . . .

'Damn!' he suddenly exploded. 'How *could* I have left that last putt short!'

Martha closed her eyes in exasperation. 'Honestly Henry! How can you let such meaningless things depress you? You haven't robbed a church or set fire to a nursing home. You only missed a silly little putt on a beautiful springtime day.'

Then, as if the wisdom of her words had washed away his golfing blues, she turned her thoughts back to Katie.

'I'm worried about her, Henry. She's become an absolute recluse. A girl her age needs companionship. On such. a gorgeous day as this, why is she down there in the basement instead of going out with her friends?'

'Katie's just different,' he said. 'Like Einstein and Edison were different. Her IQ practically zooms right off the Richter scale or whatever it is they measure geniuses on.' As unobtrusively as possible he glanced at his watch. There still were a few minutes to go until the final round of the Masters came on television. 'Katie's won first prize in the city-wide Junior Science Fair each of the last two years,' he reminded Martha. 'Right now, all she's interested in is getting ready for the same competition next month.'

'Well, I think we should go to Europe if for no other reason than to let Katie stay with Gina Wulf for those three weeks. Gina has oodles of friends and ... Henry why on earth do you keep peeking at your watch?'

'It's time for the Masters.'

'You mean Melanie and Sid are dropping by?'

'No, no, Martha. I mean the golf-tournament Masters. It's just about to come on television.'

Martha said nothing. She simply heaved a despairing sigh. In the chilly silence Henry excused himself, hastened into the den and switched on the TV. He suspected that with golf as his mistress he was hardly the world's most attentive husband. He should tell Martha more often how very much she meant to him.

In another few minutes Phil Mickelson was stroking a five-foot putt. When it lipped the cup and stayed out, Henry's psyche perked up considerably. Hell, the putt he himself had missed today on the eighteenth green had seemed more difficult than that!

Now Henry's attention focused on a player of more mellow vintage, Fred Couples, who still could move the ball as far as many of the younger pros, his swing as relaxed as if he were catching butterflies. A few of Henry's brain cells sprang to attention. *Ah, Henry, so that's the key! Not just blind confidence or the position of your hands at impact but how well you relax! No wonder you screwed up today – you were too damn tense. Next time if you take it smooth and easy like Fred Couples, won't all those other elements fall naturally into place?...*

When the televised tournament ended Henry switched off the set, lost for what to do next. Should he seek out Martha and apologize for his earlier lack of attention? Or should he pay a visit to his twelve-year-old daughter in the basement? Why did he keep dodging the fact that being an attentive husband and father was vastly more important than becoming a good golfer? And for him a far more attainable goal. Henry kicked one foot against the other in disgust. Who was he kidding to believe that from today's television viewing he had at last unlocked the secret to better golf? Wasn't he only continuing to delude himself with wishful thinking? Didn't every hard bit of evidence point to the fact – as it always had – that his game was only going to grow progressively worse?

Henry leaned forward on the sofa and buried his face in his hands. Ten, fifteen, perhaps twenty minutes later a startling idea began to germinate in his mind, gradually spreading in waves from one end of his cranium to the other, sometimes diminishing in intensity only to come pounding forward again stronger than ever. At last he lifted his head, squared his shoulders and pursed his lips with determination. The thought that pervaded him was so staggering in its implications and yet so logically sound that he wondered why it had eluded him until now.

Suddenly he was on his feet, leaping up the stairs to the bedroom where his wife, seated on the chaise-longue, looked up from her book with a start.

'Europe should be fun,' Henry heard himself say. 'I'll get my passport picture taken tomorrow.'

Martha's expression grew into one of disbelieving elation. 'Henry? What's come over you?'

'I just think we'll enjoy Europe together, that's all. France, Britain, Italy, Austria –you name it.' When she only continued to stare back at him with a mixture of alarm and amazement, he finally dropped his eyes. For some time he made arcs on the bedroom carpet with the toe of his shoe. 'I've been a negligent husband,' he managed finally. 'Maybe I can show you that, deep down, I'm really not such a bad guy after all.' Henry paused in order to afford his next words the impact they deserved. '*I'm giving up the game, Martha. As of now, I'm a non-golfer, period.*'

'Henry!'

'That's it, sweetheart. No ifs, ands or buts. That's it!' Henry felt strangely giddy as he began pacing the room, only vaguely mindful that his wife was suggesting a less drastic course of action. Like continuing to play two or three times a month just for fun and fresh air. He whirled around, interrupting her.

'It doesn't work that way,' he said. 'Golf isn't some funky little thing like bridge or Mah Jong. It's a goddamn addiction.'

18

Henry resumed pacing. 'By God, I can do it.' His voice rang with such conviction that he could hardly believe it was his own. 'As of this moment, I, Henry D. Summerfill, am an ex-golfer, period.'

'That's very admirable, dear. But shouldn't you have made that decision last month before we invited the Dunstans to the Roundup?'

Henry stopped circling the room and frowned. Good Lord, how could he have forgotten the Roundup? It was the big golf and social event in May – a two-day member-guest tournament at the club followed by a Saturday-night dinner-dance. In another three weeks Bob and Janet Dunstan would be arriving from Milwaukee. Bob had been Henry's good college friend and captain of the golf team. Since he was still an excellent golfer, Henry had been delighted to recruit a partner of such calibre. And he had been equally delighted – even if wickedly so – that Bob's wife Janet would be spending two nights under the Summerfill roof. Somehow Henry had never got round to telling Martha that Janet had been his old college flame. Through the years the two couples had occasionally run into each other at college football games, and each time Janet seemed more fetching than before. In the back of his mind he had often wondered if somewhere within her voluptuous bosom an ember still flickered for good old Henry Summerfill. But, at the moment, even that thought took a back seat to his overriding resolve to give up golf once and for all.

'I'll phone Bob Dunstan tomorrow,' he almost shouted. 'I'll tell him I've broken my leg.' Henry slammed a fist into his palm with such force that he all but yelped with pain. But soon a strange serenity began to pervade his entire being.

'I may run back to the club this afternoon and clean out my locker. I know a nice little caddy who'd love to have my

19

clubs.' He wondered if he was getting carried away with his new sanctimonious attitude. 'I'll help you cross-breed your tulips and I'll lend Katie a hand on her science fair experiment and I'll . . . .'

Henry stopped in mid-sentence, ashamed to realize that in his preoccupation with golf he had not even bothered to ask his daughter the nature of her current project. A flood of compassion surfaced within him. He could see Katie now, seriously at work in the basement, caring not at all that other girls of her age sat with the phone in one hand and the TV clicker in the other, giggling and gossiping about whatever girls that age giggle and gossip about. Yes, he could see her quizzical eyes behind her large round glasses, and though she was a source of perpetual confusion to him, she was still his baby and he loved her very much.

'Look, Martha,' he said, 'why don't you get busy on the itinerary for our trip? Right now I'm anxious to find out what our little genius is up to.'

Henry bounded down to the basement, unaware that by the time he reclimbed those stairs his life would never be the same again.

4

It pleased Henry to be so genuinely welcomed into his daughter's sacred domain.

'Just a minute, Daddy, while I finish recording this data.' Despite Katie's studious expression her eyes twinkled up at him. 'Then would you like to see what I'm working on for the fair?'

'Yes, very much.' He glanced around the neon-lit basement alcove that served as Katie's laboratory, feeling almost intimidated by the array of esoteric equipment surrounding him – beakers, burners, coils, meters – all either given to her as Christmas and birthday presents, or purchased by her with money she had saved up from allowances or earned as cash prizes in the last two city-wide junior science fairs.

'How was your golf game today?' she asked, putting down her pencil. 'Last night you seemed so convinced you'd shoot the best score of your life.'

As was often the case, Henry could not determine whether or not a hint of sly humour lay in his daughter's voice. He only wished he had been more restrained in expressing his pre-game enthusiasm. Now he was forced to admit defeat.

'I just don't know what went wrong, Katie.'

His daughter nodded with solemn understanding. 'Isn't it

amazing how eye–hand coordination can be influenced by so many subjective factors!'

'Beg pardon, honey?'

'Oh, nothing.' Katie picked up her pencil to record the movement of an electronic measuring needle. 'Did you lose a lot of money again to Mr Wulf?'

'What? How did you know that?' Henry felt himself flush. 'I mean, where did you get the idea that Alex Wulf and I ...' his voice trailed off.

'Gina Wulf told me at school. She says her dad keeps referring to you as his meal-ticket.'

When Henry lowered his head and remained silent, his daughter cast him a piquant smile. 'Of course I didn't believe Gina for a minute, Daddy.' Katie moved closer, speaking just above a whisper. 'And just in case you're wondering, I'd never *ever* mention it to Mom.'

Henry still did not raise his head. 'Well, it's not that I normally keep secrets from your mother, but ... but ...'

'I understand, Daddy – you just feel that the thought of your making an occasional sporting wager might make her nervous, right?'

'Right, Katie. Yes, that's it exactly.'

As the silence closed back around them, Henry experienced an uncomfortable gnawing inside. Despite his daughter's grasp of the situation, was she by any chance wondering if he might not have bought her some much-needed piece of equipment with the money he had been donating instead to Alex Wulf? He was about to inform Katie of his sudden and prudent decision to retire from golf altogether when she turned off the electronic meter, closed her notebook and asked whether he remembered the subject of her last year's experiment for the science fair.

Henry tugged at his ear. 'Right at the moment,' he admitted, 'it escapes me.'

'Manifestations of Negative Cellular Feedback,' she announced. 'I can't believe you and Mom can't seem to remember.'

'I'll do better remembering this year's project,' he said. 'Just try me. Tell it to me one time and I'll show you I'll never forget it.'

She looked at him full in the face, forming her words carefully. 'The Effects of Inverse Sensitizers on Molecular Polarization.'

'Once more, Katie. But more slowly, please.'

She laughed gleefully as if her father had never before been exposed to the real guts of the English language. After repeating the title a second and third time, she concluded by emphasizing that she had stated the nature of her project as simply as possible and that it meant precisely what it said.

Henry tried not to hint at any confusion in his responding nod.

'Do you have anything on a display panel like last year that I can, you know, sort of look at?'

'It's not exactly a display panel but yes, it *is* something I'm prepared to demonstrate.' Katie hesitated. 'But first I owe you an apology. A couple of weeks ago I found two golf balls in a corner of your den. Mom said she didn't think you'd mind if I used them in my experiment.' Katie's eyes begged his forgiveness so effectively that he didn't have the heart to tell her that those were his indoor putting balls which he had been searching for throughout the house.

'I'm sorry, Daddy,' she was saying, 'but I desperately needed some kind of solid sphere that contained either crispolybutadiene or methacrylate, and those two golf balls seemed the cheapest and most appropriate answer.' Even

23

before finishing her apology she stepped to a table and removed a large cloth that had covered three pairs of upright Plexiglas cylinders, perhaps five feet in height, their bases attached to a wooden frame. Beside each pair of cylinders rested three pairs of balls of differing types. One of each pair was marked A, the other B.

'These are billiard balls,' said Katie, pointing to the two on the left. 'These two in the middle are hard rubber balls, and, as you can see, the ones over here are your two golf balls. Notice too, Daddy, that there are identical gradation marks on all the cylinders and that each cylinder has a little platform at the top where I rest the balls before pulling a lever. When balls A and B are released simultaneously a direct calibration can be recorded of their comparative responses.'

'What am I supposed to look for?' asked Henry.

Apparently Katie was not yet ready to answer his question. 'This is the display proof that substantiates my hypothesis,' she went on, running a loving hand over the various components of her handiwork. 'I was about to give up on the validity of the whole concept after more than three months of struggle when, whammo, just two weeks ago I had this big breakthrough. I guess I was just too stupid not to have thought of it sooner but then it suddenly occurred to me that if I employed the fractional factorial design method of elimination, I could bypass a whole series of experimental steps on a probability basis. Now I think I'm all set.'

As Katie stepped behind the table near the panel of levers Henry wondered whether a translator for her sort of language might be found in the Yellow Pages. He watched her pick up the six balls and place them one at a time on the shelves above the cylinders.

'These three balls marked A,' she explained – 'the billiard ball, the rubber ball and the golf ball – were not subjected to thermal sensitizers, either direct or inverse, or, in fact, to any kind of cellular agitation at all. On the other hand, each corresponding ball marked B has been exposed – under controlled and monitored conditions, of course – to a variety of specific impulses. Understand so far, Daddy?'

Although Henry assured his daughter he had followed her every step of the way, for all he knew he was about to witness the unveiling of nuclear hand-grenades.

'Now, Daddy, let me demonstrate the proof of my theory that the normal polarization pattern of structural molecules contained in a solid sphere can be altered by inducing certain thermal sensitizers. As you might have guessed, those sensitizers serve as the catalyst to accelerate the agitation input factor.' After waiting for his affirmative nod that it made good common sense, Katie pressed a lever at the edge of the table, releasing the two billiard balls. They dropped together into their respective Plexiglas cylinders with ball B then bounding up somewhat higher than ball A. When she next released the hard rubber balls a similar reactive pattern resulted but with a more pronounced difference.

'Okay, Daddy, now for the golf balls. I'll bet you never dreamed you'd lose two of them to the science fair.' She tripped the lever that dropped each ball down its vertical tube.

When Henry observed the behaviour of golf ball B he stared in silent amazement. Not only was its initial bounce considerably higher than that of golf ball A but it continued bouncing crisply, even though with ever-diminishing height, long after its untreated companion had given up the ghost.

Slowly at first, then with a gathering rush, Henry's mind began grasping the implications of the miracle he had just witnessed. His reaction began with a chill at the top of his scalp. In no time at all it zipped down his spine and into the far reaches of his fingertips and toes. He tried to speak but his mouth was too dry. He swallowed twice and wet his lips.

'Let me ... see that again,' he heard himself ask.

She seemed not to have heard his request. 'My goal, Daddy, is to alter equally the molecular polarization in solid spheres of varying densities. From the practical standpoint of cyberspace application, the tolerance in the control factors . . . .'

Henry's own practical standpoint differed radically from that of his daughter's.

'Katie,' he tried to break in, 'may I ...?'

'Maybe,' she continued, not listening, 'the impact resiliency of the particles breaks down the stability of . . . .'

'Katie ... Katie . . . .'

'Then too, Daddy, there comes into play a possible manifestation of the Bernoulli Effect which I'm sure you remember from college.'

'Uh-huh . . .' Frankly, Henry didn't give a damn about the Bernoulli Effect or any of those other weird things she kept talking about. He was interested solely in the possibility of a brand new Summerfill Effect on the Rolling Hills golf-course. Altogether forgetting his recent masterful renunciation of the game in the presence of his wife, he waited till Katie was forced to take another breath, then all but shouted into her ear: 'Katie, may I borrow golf ball B for a couple of hours? I'd like to run a little experiment of my own.'

Rather than seeming to heed his question she stared at him in alarm. 'Are you all right, Daddy? You're shaking all over.'

'I'm – I'm all right,' he managed. 'All I want is . . . .'

'Even your eyes are rolling. I think I'd better call Mom.'

'Katie, no. Definitely not that.' He attempted a calm, healthy smile by way of convincing his daughter he had never been in such a sound state of mind and body. 'May I b-borrow the ball now,' he asked as gently as he was able, 'p-please?'

'Borrow it! ... But why?'

'Well, I – uh – I thought I might take it to the golf course and – uh – hit it. You know. Just out of curiosity.'

'What if you lost it, Daddy? Where would I be then? I just don't have time to go through the whole formulating process again.'

'Oh, I wouldn't lose it, honey.' He extended her a gaze of unquestionable sincerity. 'Impossible.'

'That word is the greatest fallacy in the world, Daddy. The impossible happens all the time.' Her eyes shone with compassion through her thick-lensed glasses. 'Sorry,' she said.

In the silence that followed Henry finally reached out to caress golf ball B with his fingertips as if it were some unattainable star in the firmament. When he spoke he tried to muster all the persuasiveness at his command.

'Just suppose, OK? that a ball like this could cause me to play much better golf. I mean, if I could hit it further, doesn't it stand to reason I could considerably lower my score? And if I scored a lot better – or even just a little better – I could start winning those – ah – modest sporting wagers from Gina Wulf's daddy. Who knows? – maybe it wouldn't be long before I could afford to buy my lovely, talented daughter some real goodies in the way of new laboratory equipment.'

For almost a minute they stared at each other without speaking, only fencing with their eyes, each gradually generating the slyest of smiles until they both laughed aloud and hugged one another.

'OK, Daddy. I'll make you a deal. You can hit this ball for a little while but you've got to take me with you. I just can't afford to lose it.'

In no time at all Henry called up to the bedroom from the front hall.

'Oh, Martha, Katie's going to run over to the club with me for a few minutes.'

'But Henry, it's already past five. Aren't you forgetting we're to be at a cocktail party by six-thirty?'

'Don't worry,' he shouted, reaching for the door. 'We'll be back soon.' But before he had managed his exit his wife was sending another message down the staircase.

'When you give your clubs to that caddy, Henry dear, be sure to bring home your golf umbrella.' Her voice rose musically. 'We just might need it for our very first rain in Spain.'

5

Martha hummed to herself – a bit off-key but a bona fide hum nonetheless – as she opened the deepest drawer in her desk and pulled forth a handful of well-worn travel folders. At last Henry had promised to take her to Europe! After glancing out of the window at her well-manicured rose garden she again reclined on the *chaise-longue* and began thumbing through a brochure that extolled the chateau country in France.

How marvellous that her years of golf widowhood had finally come to an end! From this point forward perhaps Henry would be on hand to change a light bulb or fetch potting compost for her plants. He might even begin to notice when she wore a new dress or came home with a different hair-do. Best of all he might remember when she'd advised him that they had been invited out for the evening. As it was, he never failed to insist with a frown, as he donned a clean shirt, that he couldn't recall her ever having mentioned it at all. How, Martha wondered, could Henry have remained so unaware of all that was commonplace around him and yet, with no effort whatsoever, recall in maddening detail every bit of golfing trivia he had ever heard, read, seen or experienced?

She almost grew angry at the thought of how the game of

golf had influenced his moods and habits all these past years. Whenever he had returned home from the club he had either barged through the door as buoyant as a schoolboy if he had played well, or as tired and crotchety as an octogenarian if he had played poorly. Unfortunately the latter had generally been the rule rather than the exception. And recently that rule had been proving itself nearly one hundred per cent of the time. The upshot was that the more his game had slid downhill the more frantically he had tried to improve it.

He had read, underlined and catalogued every golfing magazine that was ever published and he had ordered every gadget advertised in their pages. He could easily have conducted the first Golfers Only garage sale in history and realized enough income from it to buy her a whole wardrobe of designer clothes. Instead the magazines and the gadgets, along with dozens of once-tried putters, remained scattered around the premises. Not only were they irritating reminders of his expensive hobby but hazards to her safety each time she walked into a darkened room.

Yes, Henry had phrased it correctly this afternoon when he had finally faced up to the fact that golf had been his vice and addiction. And yet, as a woman of strict Episcopalian upbringing, Martha had at least been grateful that her Henry was not the type to ogle shapely young girls or gamble for money.

She gazed again at the folder in her lap. Europe in June – only another seven weeks from this very moment! She could see Henry now with that sweet shy smile once again on his face, a convert to old-world antiquities, standing in rapt attention before the Mona Lisa, silently asking himself why he had ever let himself become so captivated by golf when the Louvre had been waiting for him all these years. And that evening as they dined alone in a Left Bank candle-lit café it would be like honeymooning all over again.

When the bedside clock caught her eye she leaped to her feet and started at once to dress for the cocktail party. Why hadn't Henry and Katie yet returned? Ten minutes later her nervousness increased to such a point that she phoned the pro shop at the club to ask whether Henry hadn't yet finished cleaning out his locker. But the phone rang unanswered. If the place was already locked up, where could the two of them be? So often when they were together they behaved like a pair of children off on a magic carpet to Never-Never Land . . . . *Honestly!*

Long after Martha was dressed she paced the floor, gazing out of the front window as the chill of twilight settled over the world. Her impatience grew into annoyance, then finally into a growing fear that her husband and daughter had met with some unusual calamity.

6

Late afternoon shadows had already stretched themselves across the fairways of the Rolling Hills Country Club when Henry Summerfill zoomed his car through the club gate.

'Now, Katie,' he cautioned. 'This matter of the – uh – slightly modified golf ball is just between you and me, OK?'

'OK, Daddy.'

A few minutes later, after Henry's clubs had been delivered to the first tee on a cart, he was relieved to find the course deserted. Even Jeff Logan, the club pro, had left for the day. Henry removed his driver from his bag and hurriedly set about loosening up with a few practice swings. He peered over his shoulder to make sure no one was watching, then whispered to Katie to hand him the ball. He teed it up with trembling fingers, staring down at it as if his entire future lay within the confines of its white, dimpled cover. What, he wondered, was about to happen?

He admonished himself to relax as he took his stance. For what seemed an eternity he stood above the ball like a robot, attempting to programme each of his muscles to coordinate with the others when he set his swing into motion. At last his club began moving away from the ball, not with the rhythmic ease he had hoped for but instead with a jerk. His downswing began even before his backswing was completed, all but whiplashing his wrists. When the club-head met the ball with maximum effort but with minimum force he knew he had muffed the shot. He looked up in despair to find the ball bounding forward from the tee, refusing to get airborne. Although he could not see beyond where the fairway sloped downwards shortly past the tee, he knew it wouldn't travel nearly as far as his morning's drive, which had come to rest opposite the first big tree on the left. But after he had climbed into the golf cart beside Katie and started off in pursuit, he was amazed to discover that the ball was not there in the centre of the fairway where he had expected to find it. Was it possible, he thought with a shudder, that it had disintegrated completely? And Katie grew equally nervous as they kept driving in ever-widening circles with nothing in sight but two squirrels who couldn't have cared less.

'Hey, Daddy, look!' Katie pointed to a white speck perhaps another eighty yards down the sloping fairway.

'No, that couldn't be it. That's just a piece of paper.' But even as Henry spoke he aimed the cart in its direction. A strange lump rose in his throat as he found himself crazily and illogically hoping that his daughter might be right after all.

The closer they approached, the rounder the object grew in appearance. Henry squinted in all directions to make sure that the ball, if such it really could be, was not the result of an extremely wild shot by another golfer who, by chance, might still be out on the course. But no one was visible. As far as Henry could see there were only Katie and himself, the two squirrels, and now this marvellous gleaming sphere. He jolted the cart to a stop beside the ball and leaped out to inspect it. When he detected a large B scrawled by a felt pen his spirit seemed to leave his body and float high above the crisp green fairway. Good Lord, his weakly topped drive had travelled half as far again as his well-hit shot on the same hole earlier in the day!

'I don't understand it,' he muttered over and over again.

'It's very simple, Daddy,' said a voice from the world of reality. 'The sensitized molecular particles reagitate themselves each time the ball bounces. That gives it a new burst of energy – sort of like booster rockets on a spaceship – until finally the friction of grass and air cause it to stop.'

When Henry felt his feet make contact with the turf again he couldn't wait to hit his next shot. But what club to use? His drive had never before ended up so close to the green, perhaps only 130 yards away, right up there where the young sluggers hit their shots. After considerable debate he selected a seven-iron, refusing from past experience to believe it possible to reach the green with any club of greater loft.

'You're getting too jumpy,' his daughter said. 'Just take some deep breaths . . . . No, no, Daddy, not fast ones. You're not drowning. Do it slow.'

Although Henry recognized the validity of his daughter's advice he couldn't wait to get on with the show. He addressed the ball quickly and swung through the shot with a surprising feeling of tempo and firmness. The instant he spotted his ball in flight he knew he should have selected a shorter-distance club. With a mixture of glorious amazement and abject horror he watched the ball sail over the green to light on a bench beside the second tee, bounding again to land a second time on the tarmac road just outside the club property. Finally, according to Katie, it splashed into the creek on the far side of the road.

Henry remained grimly silent as they sped in the cart towards the scene of disaster. He wished for a siren so that the trees in their path might move aside to let them pass. From the corner of his eye he saw Katie clinging to the cart seat beside him, her face horror-struck, no less panicky than he as to whether they stood even the slimmest chance of recovering the world's most astounding golf ball.

For the next half-hour the two of them edged their way up and down the bank of the creek, dipping into its murky depths with Henry's irons, seeking to dredge out the ball.

'It's just got to be further out in the water,' said Katie, half wailing. 'We'll have to go in after it.'

But already Henry had discarded his shoes and socks and rolled his trouser legs above his knees. He edged down the bank into the water, catching his breath from its chill. He had taken only two exploratory steps when he found himself submerged to the waist. Together Katie and he began a systematic search with their toes. When the sun slid from sight Henry's shivering became more pronounced.

'Hey there, are you all right?'

Henry peered through the dusk at the motorist who had pulled to the side of the road.

'Yes, thanks, we're f-fine.'

'If you're trying to catch frogs, it's a little early in the year.'

'It's just that we're looking for something rather important.'

The motorist hesitated. 'You're not dredging for a body, are you?'

'Daddy lost my golf ball,' shouted Katie, not looking up.

The man only stared in disbelief, then drove off shaking his head. Other motorists paused too, some to enquire, some only to gape, and one to clamber from his car, attach an electronic flash to his camera and shoot a roll of film. Despite Henry's shivers turning into shakes he held no thought of giving up the quest. He only wondered absently what time it was getting to be as he continued sweeping his feet across the muddy creek bed.

Katie's whimpers grew in frequency and volume.

'We've got to find it, Daddy. I just can't let my whole year's experiment go down the drain this way.'

'Let's keep calm, honey. Remember, when the going gets tough, the tough get going.' Henry had to admit that his favourite motto seemed a bit obscure for the situation in hand, but what else was there to say? He wished the U.S. Navy would arrive with a flotilla of underwater-search gear, and not fail to bring along arctic-water togs for the crew. Soon Henry's toes would be too desensitized to feel themselves banging against a rock.

'Hey, you ... hey, what are you doing there?'

Henry glanced up at the sound of an authoritative voice. Two policemen stood on the creek bank. The blinking red light on top of their patrol car attracted other motorists who now stopped to witness at closer range whatever drama was unfolding.

'We're only l-l-looking for a g-g-golf ball, officer.'

'Sure you are mister .... Come over here and keep your hands above your head. The same goes for your girlfriend too.'

Henry found it difficult to sound offended through chattering teeth. 'Th-that h-happens to be my d-d-daughter.'

'Golly, officers,' said Katie, 'you're public servants, aren't you? Why can't you help us? This is a very special ball we've lost. If the same principle were applied to the lag phase of the duo-rectifier in a space command module, it could save the taxpayers enough money to double the salary of every policeman like you in the country.'

The officers turned slowly to stare at each other, then just as slowly turned back towards the odd couple in the water.

'I thought I told you to come over here,' said the larger of the two patrolmen as a growing crowd of onlookers formed a

36

tighter semicircle around them.

'All right, folks,' said the other policeman. 'Just step back, please. We don't want anyone getting hurt.'

'Hey!' Henry suddenly shouted. 'I may have found it.' He plunged an arm deep into the water, his face submerging in the process. In another moment he held up a golf ball covered with mud. 'Say, officer,' called Henry, 'c-could you flash your light here f-for a second? I can't read the m-m-marking on this b-b-b-ball.'

The officer shook his head in confusion, stepped to the patrol car, snapped on a spotlight and aimed its beam towards the object in Henry's hand.

'Eureka!' cried Henry. 'This is it!'

'I think they've struck gold,' said a voice in the crowd.

When Henry and Katie in turn planted a shivering kiss on the mud-soaked ball a rousing cheer rose from the throng.

Totally out of character but too happy to care, Henry removed his glasses, shook back his wet hair and opened his arms to them all. It was then that he saw in the midst of the crowd a shocked, familiar face staring deeply into his eyes.

Henry struggled to assume a more dignified countenance.

'M-M-Martha,' he heard himself mutter, 'how g-good of you to c-c-come!'

7

'Oh, Charlotte,' said Henry at two o'clock the next afternoon.
'I've been called out of the office for the rest of the day.'
Between sneezes he pretended to arrange papers on his desk.
Although he frequently shared his golfing exploits with his
primly efficient secretary – even to the point of embellishing
a bit on his prowess – he felt it not quite fitting to reveal that
he was taking the greater part of Monday afternoon off to
sneak away to the golf-course.

'I do hope you're not catching cold, Mr Summerfill. If your
wife calls, what shall I tell her?'

Henry sneezed twice before answering.

'Just say I'm at a meeting, Charlotte, and that I should be
home at the regular time.' Henry wondered if guilt showed
on his face. Monday was the one day of the week that even
the most ardent businessman golfer stayed on the job. For one
thing, he would have played only yesterday. For another, the
private courses in the area were closed to general play on
Mondays. Henry gazed up and down the corridor to make
sure his colleagues had their faces buried in desk work. Then,
as carefully as defusing a bomb, he unlocked his desk drawer,
retrieved a small black box from under a sheaf of papers,
withdrew from it a green felt pouch containing golf ball B and

left the office as unobtrusively as possible. But he was careful to pretend by his manner that he was only stepping out for a moment to buy a tin of aspirin.

As he drove towards the club, trying not to flagrantly exceed the speed limit, he scolded himself for having been so impetuous as to have announced to Martha that he had decided to give up golf altogether. Of course that was before his awareness of Katie's scientific bonanza which had led to his wife's being a witness to the fiasco in the creek. That in turn had led to her bedtime diagnosis that his brain had indeed snapped and shouldn't he make an appointment with a psychiatrist who specialized in compulsive golf maniacs? As was always the case when he found himself on his wife's witness stand, he had been hard pressed to pull together any plausible defense, especially at the time of night that seemed to be her strongest verbal-assault hour and his own weakest. But under no circumstances had he considered divulging the miraculous truth. The last thing he wanted was for his wife to phone the news to the whole world by nine the next morning. The best he had managed was to say he had been unable to invent any valid excuse to give Bob Dunstan for pulling out of the Roundup. As a follow-up he recited back her own suggestion that instead of his giving up the game completely he should keep playing occasionally for fun and fresh air.

She had drawn herself up to her full height which, unfortunately, somewhat exceeded his own. 'By fun and fresh air,' she said, 'I was not implying that you should take your daughter wading in a freezing creek after dark. And with all those people watching your silly antics! *Honestly*, Henry!' He had then sat mutely on the edge of the bed staring absently at his toes waiting for her to say *Honestly*, Henry! a few more times before she snapped off the light and arranged herself as precariously as she dared on her side of the bed without falling off.

But those recollections of last night flew from Henry's mind as swiftly as bats from a cave when he screeched his car to a halt in the parking lot at Rolling Hills. After quickly changing clothes he jumped into a golf cart and sped to the deserted practice tee far removed from the clubhouse. Here, in this broad, treeless area, with no out-of-bounds within a quarter of a mile, he was safe in resuming his experiment with golf ball B without fear of its becoming lost. And he was especially grateful that Katie had agreed to let him practise with it one more time in return for his promise to buy her a new supply of beakers. But the arrangement was only a temporary stop-gap at best. He would have to talk to her as soon as possible about her furnishing him with a workable supply.

Henry resented having to take time to limber up with a few practice swings but if he failed to do so he realized he might end up with a sprung fifth vertebra or a double hernia. While it was going to seem like such a frustrating waste of time to hit the ball, retrieve it in his cart, and then drive back to the practice tee before hitting it again, he consoled himself in the awareness that one such ball was infinitely better than none. He took two more practice swings, then declared himself ready.

Henry's first order of business was to hit three ordinary balls so that he could establish some measurement of the relative difference in distance between those balls and his scientifically modified ball – a Top Flite. After driving three regular balls, all of which proved to be good straight shots of perhaps 180 yards, Henry prepared to shoot his miracle ball. His heart pounded in his chest as he checked out the components of his stance, took a deep breath, then swept through his swing, making firm contact with the club-face. He tingled with elation to watch the ball soar like a white dove into the

April sky, at last returning to earth to begin bounding forwards until it came to rest well beyond 200 yards. Good Lord, he had never hit a ball so far in his life!

After staring down the practice fairway for a full minute in stunned silence he leaped into the golf cart, racing to retrieve the ball as if seeking the world's speed record on the Bonneville salt flats. He swooped up the ball and returned to the tee where he repeated his magnificent feat time after time. At last he clenched his fists and gave vent to a laugh reeking with sadistic glee.

'Alex Wulf, you big sonofabitch, here I come.' Never had Henry felt so strong, so macho!

But scoring at golf, he reminded himself, was not simply a matter of booming drives. There was more work to be done. He steered his cart to a point 150 yards from the practice green to determine which of his irons was most suited for propelling his miracle ball that specified distance. After several such shots, most of which ended up over the green, he settled on his seven-iron which lofted the ball just short of the green where it hopped briskly on to the putting surface. By this process of trial and error he discovered yet another characteristic of the ball. Despite its strong bounding quality on the fairway, it settled down to a normal roll once it reached the smooth surface of the green. But when he decided to see if it responded any differently with a putter he suffered his first setback. Time and again the ball rolled so strongly past the hole that Henry concluded its response was just too lively for such a delicate stroke. He tried to swallow his disappointment philosophically – if someone gave you the moon, should you expect to be handed the stars as well? And didn't almost everyone use a separate ball for putting anyway? – a clean ball free from the nicks and bruises inflicted by the longer, more violent shots.

41

Henry was surprised when he glanced at his watch to find that he had been practising for more than three hours. But he felt it might just prove to be the most productive afternoon of his life.

After dinner, while Martha was on the phone discussing geraniums, Henry drew Katie aside and briefed her on his afternoon's results. He then suggested that the two of them should retreat to her laboratory. Once there Henry picked up a hammer lying on the work-bench and intermittently tapped it against a piece of wood as if signalling upstairs that he was busy helping his daughter with some construction project related to her exhibit at the science fair.

'Katie,' he said, producing the ball, 'how about fixing me up with a dozen others just like this one?'

'It's not that simple, Daddy. It's a long, tedious process. It's got to be done perfectly or it won't work at all. The thermal gradient, for instance, has to be right on the nose. The photo-cellular sensitivity reaction has to be watched every second for four hours. And the digital osmosis synthesis is touch and go throughout repeated periods of magnetic agitation.' She looked up at him through her thick-lensed glasses. 'Anyway, Daddy, I've got to keep on schedule with my experiment. The science fair is less than a month away.'

Henry frowned as he mulled over the predicament, now and then glancing towards the ceiling as if to determine whether or not his wife might have concluded her geranium conversation and was now placing a listening ear against the living-room floor. For insurance's sake, he tapped the hammer a few times against the piece of wood in his hand, then whispered to his daughter: 'I'll pay you for the balls, Katie. I mean, pay you nicely. How much do you think would be fair?'

Katie pondered his question, the wisp of a smile playing at

the corners of her mouth.

'How much is it worth to you, Daddy?'

'How about – uh – five dollars a ball?'

Katie looked back at him, shocked.

'That wouldn't even be minimum wages.'

'Maybe ten?'

'Keep going, Daddy.'

Henry could tell from the gleam in his daughter's eye that she was already enjoying this bargaining session.

'Ten dollars a ball is a lot of money for a twelve-year-old to earn,' he said. 'This could be a continuing source of revenue for you. Let's settle on ten dollars. OK?'

'Keep going,' she repeated.

Henry felt convinced that Katie was more suited to business matters than he.

'All right,' he said, 'let's not quibble. Fifteen dollars, agreed?'

'Twenty.'

'Fifteen.'

'Daddy, you're wasting my time. I've got to get on with my work.'

'Oh, all right, damnit – Oooops! Katie, I'm sorry I said that – twenty dollars it is.'

'It is, yes, for the first dozen. We'll renegotiate when you're ready for more.'

When he heard the basement door open, he quickly resumed hammering, pausing only long enough to call up the stairs, 'I'll be there in a minute, darling – just as soon as I finish this one little thing for Katie.'

After his wife's footsteps had retreated he reached for his wallet and counted out his ready-cash resources of forty-eight dollars.

'I'll pay you the rest tomorrow,' he said, then added a

personal plea. 'But could I keep just a few dollars for now? I won't have a chance to get to the bank till tomorrow afternoon, and I would like a little something for lunch.'

Later, before falling asleep, Henry wondered how much money Alex Wulf might be willing to bet on Saturday's game.

8

Henry arrived at the club on Saturday well before tee-off time. Before starting play with his regular foursome he was anxious for a few private words with club pro Jeff Logan. But he would have to be wary: he didn't want Jeff to suspect that his questions regarding golf balls were motivated by anything other than academic interest.

In the pro shop Henry pretended to peruse the sports shirts on display while Jeff Logan showed some golf gloves to Roger Martin. 'Be with you in a minute, Henry – just as soon as I get Mr Martin fixed up.'

Henry waved an amicable acknowledgement, then turned away so as not to reveal a hint of smugness in his smile. Jeff's remark may have sounded innocuous enough on the surface but to Henry it was steeped in profound undertones. Both Henry and Roger Martin were of the same vintage and yet Jeff had greeted Henry by his first name while addressing Roger as Mister. Why? Simply because the pro obviously accepted Henry as a true fraternal golfing spirit while Roger Martin had yet to attain that distinction? Of course Alex Wulf had a different theory but then Alex always delighted in pulling Henry's leg. Alex insisted that if a member's purchases from the pro shop were limited to golf balls and sundry minor equipment he remained Mister. But if his purchases exceeded a few hundred dollars a month, Jeff would bestow the status symbol of greeting him by his first name. Henry shrugged away the ridiculousness of Alex's premise. True, Henry was accustomed to buying a new set of woods and irons frequently but he refused to believe his volume of business had anything to do with Jeff's geniality.

When Bob Martin made his exit, Henry shook the young pro's hand, then bought two golf caps, a rain jacket and a dozen golf balls destined for secret treatment in his daughter's laboratory. 'These solid centre Top-Flites are different, aren't they?' he said, choosing his words carefully. 'I mean, aren't most balls still made with separate cover and core?'

'Some are and some aren't,' Jeff answered. Then because he presumed Henry was hungry for further enlightenment, the Rolling Hills pro offered a brief history of the golf ball. The first were nothing more than lumps of hardwood which bored shepherds used to knock around with their crooks. When the game became formalized in Scotland there evolved a feather-stuffed sac. This was followed by a single blob of jungle gum, or gutta-percha. Finally came the making of an elastic sphere in three parts – the core, winding and cover.

'That's how it's remained,' said Jeff, 'for a helluva lot of years. It's just been recently that engineers have come up with both one- and two-piece balls as well.'

Henry framed his next question carefully. 'I know there are specifications a ball must conform to in size and weight and, I guess, velocity. But how can they measure the velocity performance of each and every ball?'

'You know about Mechanical Mike, don't you, Henry?'

'Oh, is he the guy who fixes broken-down golf carts?'

Jeff chuckled at Henry's apparent naïvety, then launched into an explanation of the complex testing-machine at the headquarters of the United States Golf Association in Far Hills, New Jersey.

'Mechanical Mike emulates a golfer's swing and can be calibrated so precisely that it knows how to detect an illegal ball. That's a ball that exceeds 250 feet per second coming off a club-face. You see, Henry, all golf-ball manufacturers must submit representative balls for testing all the time. The procedure is so foolproof that you can be sure any ball that reaches your hands conforms to its required specifications in all respects.'

Back at his locker, Henry was glad he had discussed the issue with Jeff Logan in such a forthright manner. The last thing Henry would want to do was to circumvent any USGA policy governing the grand old game of golf.

As he waited by the tee for his first competitive round with his miracle ball he could only hope the other three members of his group would conclude that he had simply discovered a new key to his swing that added considerable distance to his shots. Actually, mused Henry, the ball's flight in the air was not that dramatically different – its real additional distance came from its extended but less obvious overspin after hitting the turf.

A few minutes later, for the first time in Henry's memory, his drive on the first hole ended up closer to the green than any other ball of the foursome.

'My God!' cried Alex. 'What did my little buddy have for breakfast, the raw meat of a lion?'

The words spun deliciously in Henry's ears, then permeated his entire being. When he addressed his ball for his approach shot to the green he felt strangely confident that he would execute it successfully. And he did. As the round continued Henry felt himself contacting the ball more solidly and with less effort than ever before. Even his playing-mates began to behold him with awe, commenting on the new smoothness of his swing. Soon Henry himself began to wonder if the added distance of his shots was perhaps more attributable to his new-found rhythm than to the unusual properties of the ball itself. And, thankfully, not one of his group suspected otherwise.

Although Henry continued to come up with a generous share of non-spectacular shots he supposed that in the long run it was all for the best. No mediocre golfer could become an overnight sensation without others ferreting a little too deeply as to how and why. What's more, his few sand shots were just as atrocious as ever and his putting just as shaky. On one occasion he forgot to switch balls after reaching a green and putted his miracle ball. It ended up as far past the hole as it had been before attempting the twenty-foot putt. Despite having been subjected to Alex Wulf's doubling up with laughter, when Henry walked off the eighteenth green he had carded an eighty-six – his lowest score of the season.

He drove away from the club car park with a Cheshire-cat grin and a fattened wallet. It was a circumstance he would have felt more guilty about if his balance of payments over the past several seasons had not been so weighted against him. But when such twinges of guilt now and then tried to worm their way into his conscience, he chose to disregard their presence by conjuring up visions of even greater future glories. With more practice he would learn the better to handle his chipping with the lively ball. And to improve his shots from the sand, he would sign up for lessons with Jeff Logan and spend whatever time it took to master that phase of his game. But Henry's high hopes of now becoming one of Rolling Hill's top golfers started to wane when he considered the sad state of his putting. No doubt about it, it was growing worse with every round, and he could not think of a way to reverse that dismal trend. But somewhere, there just had to be a solution.

9

That evening in the seclusion of his daughter's basement laboratory Henry delivered her the new batch of Top-Flites that he had purchased from Jeff Logan. After gaining Katie's assurance that at least three more of the balls would soon be converted for his use, he slipped her the remaining healthy sum of cash he owed in return for this specialized service. They both agreed that the transaction in no way constituted a bribe on the one hand nor a pay-off on the other, but instead only a mutually agreeable means of funding Katie's continuing scientific endeavours for the benefit of all mankind. With this bit of clearing-of-the-conscience behind them, Henry felt the time had come to advance another suggestion.

'Katie, I wonder if it mightn't be more feasible for you to switch to some sphere other than a golf ball as part of your display at the science fair.' He placed a paternal arm around her shoulder. 'It just doesn't seem to be the sort of object that would impress the judges with the extent of your professionalism. I mean, a golf ball lacks scientific credibility, don't you think?'

Katie picked up a beaker, seeming to study its shape.

'What are you trying to tell me, Daddy?'

'Well, honey, in addition to the obviously valid point I just

50

made, it's possible that some busybody attending the science fair might, you know, try to put two and two together.'

When Katie only stared blankly back at him, Henry was forced to state his argument more definitively.

'Let's look at it this way,' he said, coughing slightly. 'What if some friend of your mother – or for that matter, your mother herself – should observe the behaviour of those golf balls marked A and B. The very next day she might unwittingly pass the word on to someone like – well, let's say like Alex Wulf, who had just recently seen me hit the same brand of golf ball a lot further than ever before in my life. Coincidences like that can happen, you know.'

'The Watergate plumbers should have had you on their team, Daddy. They'd never have got caught.'

'Oh, now, honey, surely you're not categorizing your father as ... as ... .'

Henry breathed more easily when Katie broke into a slow, teasing smile. 'No, of course I didn't mean it that way. Actually, Daddy, I see you as a man just freshly caught up in the cause of science – a man anxious to help his daughter by quietly augmenting a practical application of her strictly academic hypothesis.'

'Right, Katie, right, I couldn't have expressed it better myself.' He pushed back a wisp of hair from her forehead and patted her cheek. 'When you first showed me your display, you mentioned that the two golf balls weren't interacting – hey, your poppa's really learning the jargon, isn't he? – weren't interacting as consistently as the rubber balls and billiard balls.' In his mood of nothing's-too-good-for-my-daughter he then promised to buy her a pair of any other kind of solid ball she desired – even if made of gold – to replace Top-Flites A and B. When she agreed to his suggestion he could not have been more pleased.

With no further business to be taken care of at the moment Henry reached for one of the new Top-Flites that had just been delivered. He placed it on the basement floor and, as if putting, tapped it with the head of a hammer towards the leg of one of Katie's laboratory benches. The ball rolled straight and true, bumping lightly against the centre of the table-leg. He put two more balls on the floor, hitting each with the hammer head and achieving the identical perfect result.

He rose from his crouched position, rubbed the stiffness from his back and turned to his daughter with a wistful sigh.

'I wish I could be that accurate with my putter.'

'No way, Daddy.'

'OK, so I'm a lousy putter,' he said, frowning. 'What else is new?'

'Oh, I didn't mean that personally. It's just that nobody – not even the best of the pros – could putt as accurately with a normal length club as they could put with one the length of that hammer.'

'You're not often wrong about things, Katie, but I'm afraid you are this time. Otherwise, why wouldn't golfers use little short putters?'

'Because I presume they're illegal.'

'Not at all. There's no restriction as to the shaft-length of any club.'

Katie had been washing out some test-tubes as they chatted. Now she stopped to face her father in disbelief.

'You've gotta be kidding, Daddy.'

'I'm not kidding. And just why do you find that so strange?'

'Because it doesn't make good scientific sense, that's why.' She took the hammer from his hand and rested its head on the surface of the table while tilting its handle upright. For a while she gazed past his shoulder as if seeking a means of translating her thoughts into phraseology her father might comprehend.

'I want you to visualize a right-angled triangle, Daddy. This handle of the hammer is its vertical side. The tabletop is its horizontal or bottom side. That leaves the hypotenuse. You follow?'

'I follow.'

'Good. We'll take it one step further. Archimedes first established that the margin of error, when applied to any fulcrumatic mechanical function, diminishes in direct ratio to the square root of the hypotenuse. Agreed?'

'Uh, yes. Naturally.'

'OK, now let's visualize this same right-angled triangle with its three points representing your eye, the ball and the target. Angle A, of course, remains constant. But Angle B becomes greater as the hypotenuse shortens. In consequence there is less toleration of variance in pin-pointing angle C.'

'Angle C?'

'The hole in the green, Daddy. Golly, aren't you listening?'

'Of course I'm listening. It's just that it's been some time since I browsed over any geometry books.'

'All right,' said Katie as patiently as possible, 'let's forget theoretical validation. What I've been trying to tell you is that there are two reasons why an extremely short-shafted putter makes sense. First, it behaves exactly like a fulcrum. The longer it is, the more leverage you get, the shorter it is, the more delicate its response. And isn't that what putting is all about – sensitivity rather than power? Secondly, Daddy, when your eyes and hands are right down there near the ball, all three combine to form a single coordinated unit. Aiming the putt and sensing its distance becomes a breeze compared with the way it's done when the eyes and the hands and the ball are so far removed from each other.' Katie shook her head in disbelief. 'I still can't believe that you golfers haven't figured that out.'

Henry gazed heavenwards by way of asking whether his daughter was completely out of her skull or whether she had been brought into this world to solve all his golfing woes. Had he simply been short-sighted these past years in having taken lessons from Jeff Logan instead of from little Kathryn Ann Summerfill who had never held a club in her life?

At nine the next morning Henry excused himself from a business meeting long enough to phone the pro shop to ask for his putter to be cut down from its present thirty-five-inch length to twenty-two inches.

'Beg pardon?' said the assistant pro who had answered. 'I must have misunderstood you.'

Henry repeated his request two more times. After a long pause at the other end of the line he heard: 'OK, Mr Summerfill, if that's what you want, that's what you'll get.'

'Can you have it ready right after lunch?' Henry asked. 'I just may be able to break away from the office for some early afternoon putting practice.'

A few hours later in the men's grill Henry downed a chicken sandwich in half a dozen fast bites, then hurried to the practice putting-green where he dropped a pair of regular balls about five feet from the hole. The distance had always been a crucial one for him. Any golfer who repeatedly missed putts under six feet could never hope for low scores no matter how far he hit his tee ball. He was thankful no one was around to observe his pilot test, especially since the twenty-two-inch putter in his hand basically resembled a foreshortened medieval weapon. At last he crouched over the ball, trying to fit his body into a comfortable stance. He realized his rear was pointing up towards the fluffy springtime clouds in a most undignified posture but that was a compromise to athletic grace he would just have to live with. Getting on with the business in hand he took aim and tapped the ball. When it rolled into the hole as if it had eyes he felt a smile curl the corners of his lips. He then putted the second ball with the same gorgeous result. It was a godsend that he could switch to an ordinary ball for putting. Lord knows where his doctored Top-Flites might have ended up!

Time after time, from various distances and directions, Henry astounded himself with his new putting skill. And, surprisingly, even on putts of thirty feet he never failed to move the ball to within a foot or two of the hole. He wondered if Christopher Columbus had shared this same thrill of discovery when first sighting America. Out of all the millions of golfers in the world, why hadn't this miracle been chanced upon before? As Katie had maintained, it all made such obvious sense. Rather than standing high above a tiny ball, trying to manipulate its path and speed almost as if by remote control, he was now right down there where the action was, sighting behind the ball as if aiming a rifle.

Was this wholly new approach to putting destined to revolutionize the game of golf? Would there, some day, near the fringe of this practice-green at Rolling Hills, be a plaque – or perhaps even a shrine – commemorating the spot where the Summerfill technique of putting gave birth to the biggest breakthrough in the history of the sport? While he had yet to initiate his new method under competition when the pressure was on and with Alex Wulf threatening to goose him just as Henry was set to tap the ball, he could hardly wait for the weekend to roll around. Meantime, his wisest course of action was to resume practising.

After another fifteen minutes of uncomfortable crouching Henry had to concede that his new putting style posed one rather disturbing problem. In that he was obliged to assume a stance not unlike that of a linesman in football, his back came under constant and repeated strain. Following every few putts he was forced to stand erect, push his palms against his lower back and then press it forward in a bow in an effort to realign several vertebrae into their destined relationship.

It was not until the next day, however, that its full impact caught up with him. Martha cancelled her morning appointments to drive him to a chiropractor who managed to partially readjust his spine.

'I hope you've learned your lesson,' she said, driving him home. 'Surely you're never going to use that silly little putter again.'

'I just practised with it too long all at one time,' he defended.

'Really, Henry, how can you be such a masochist!'

'I'm not a masochist. It's just that the Roundup is almost here and I refuse to handicap myself with one of those old-fashioned long-handled putters.' Henry tried to hide a wince when the car hit a bump. Then he turned to his wife with a solemn vow.

'I'm going to bring home that trophy, sweetheart. And you can fill it with dahlias to your heart's content. How's that for a thoughtful husband?'

She glanced at him as if he were less of a thoughtful husband than an obstinate little boy. She rolled her eyes heavenwards.

'Honestly, Henry!' she said at last . . . . 'I mean, *honestly*!'

10

On the night before Bob and Janet Dunstan were to arrive for the Rolling Hills Roundup, Henry lay awake beside his sleeping wife. He turned his head towards the bedside clock, dismayed to find that another half-hour had passed since his last time-check. He wished that, like Martha, he was capable of floating away to the Land of Nod the instant his head hit the pillow. But he supposed that if he had nothing more to concern himself with than chatting with travel agents about their reservations in Europe next month he wouldn't be tossing and turning either. His own complex pursuits, however, demanded both past reflection and future planning. Like it or not Henry felt it essential to spend at least another few minutes of wakefulness in a review of the past ten days. In no time at all he disposed of stocks and bonds, almost refusing to acknowledge that his business life existed. He then dwelt for a moment on the condition of his back, pleased that it seemed to be staying in shape as long as he restricted his putting only to actual play. Next he got round to where his thoughts had been headed all along – a shot-by-shot replay of last Sunday's new record score of eighty-three.

The longer Henry mulled over that resplendent round of golf, the more he convinced himself that while his Katie-altered Top-Flite might have helped to contribute to his stellar play, wasn't it actually the harmony of his swing and his improved putting that had turned the trick? The miracle ball, he reasoned, served mainly as a psychological security blanket that kept him from flailing as in those god-awful days of the past. What could be more logical than that all his years of work and study on the game had at last jelled into a superlative cohesiveness of mind and body! After all, some people simply reached their peak later in life than others. Like General MacArthur and His Holiness the Pope and now, at long last, Summerfill.

Henry grinned in the darkness, his thoughts sweeping forward to tomorrow's first day of play in the Roundup. As he would split the fairways with his booming drives and burn up the greens with his unique stubby putter, who would be impressed most of all? No one other than his partner's wife and Henry's old flame, Janet Dunstan.

He watched the hands of the clock slip past 1.30 in the morning as he harkened back to a night in his young life when, during Thanksgiving break in college, he had visited Janet's home in a neighbouring town. To Henry she had been more than just another coed – she had been a goddess on a pedestal. Whenever he had conjured up visions of Janet offering her body to him (which he had to admit was pretty damn often), the imaginary setting was not a pile of autumn leaves or a sorority-house fire-escape. She would be reclining in a rich velvet robe. Then to the sound of muted violins and perhaps a far-away voice reciting Hindi poems, they would consummate their love-making in the manner of a high religious ceremony.

But as it turned out, the closest Henry ever came to deflowering Janet's virginity – and also, at that time, his own – was late that Thanksgiving night as the two of them lolled on an old sofa in her family's basement playroom, her parents having long since retired to bed. He was still debating with himself as to how to begin the grand seduction when Janet kicked off her shoes, inviting him to do the same. She pulled him down prone beside her and, astonishingly, directed his hand to her breast.

Ever so hesitantly Henry began trying to unbutton her blouse, each of his fingers feeling twice the size of his thumbs and capable of even less dexterity. After he had spent five minutes on the first button alone, Janet impatiently took over the task for him. With his head spinning from such unanticipated good fortune, Henry reached beneath her shoulders to unhook her bra. But he soon concluded that her mother must have fastened it with a combination lock that could be sprung only by their family doctor. Frantic with frustration, Henry attempted to hasten the process by propping Janet up into a sitting position and then spinning himself on to his knees behind her for a more direct assault upon the bra hooks. Just as he was about to uncage the sweet warmth of her breasts, his bare foot slipped into a crack of the battered sofa.

He screamed aloud as a coiled spring attacked his big toe with the ferocity of a bear trap. By the time he had managed to free it, Janet was wholly exasperated and fully clothed. And that had been that.

Two weeks later she began exclusively dating his friend Bob Dunstan, leaving Henry to wonder ever since how that night of nights might have turned out on a sofa of sturdier quality.

Now years later he recalled that it was not until that following summer in Colorado that he achieved his first copulatory victory in the back seat of a car parked on top of the Continental Divide. From that day forward he could not deny an inner pride, not only at having seduced a forty-year-old barmaid but also at the unusual height above sea level at which he had at last proved to himself his manhood. The following morning, with a topographical map spread before him, he had jotted down the elevation of the mountain pass, then added another thirty inches to allow for the distance of the car seat above the terrain. After completing the mathematics he had glowed with youthful elation – his precise screwing altitude had been 13,284 feet. While he had known there existed fact-finding organizations that published such accomplishments as the longest home run in baseball history, and the largest blue marlin caught on rod and reel, he had wished a similar tabulation might record the highest piece of tail captured in the northern hemisphere.

Looking back on it now, it suddenly occurred to Henry that he might have set one other record on that same long-ago night – his actual penile victory march terminated almost before it had begun. But maybe that could be blamed on the same principle that caused bacon to fry faster at high altitudes!

He had assumed that between then and now his carnal appetite would have progressively diminished. But quite the reverse had happened. While Martha's hormones seemed content to keep cool and collected, his own now swarmed more restlessly and with even greater confusion than in those days of his bumbling youth. A bit of lust crept into Henry's thoughts as he envisaged Janet Dunstan occupying an adjacent bedroom the following evening. And solely for the sake of day-dreaming convenience he chose to disregard that her husband would be there too. But before he allowed his imagination to wander indiscriminately off on that particular sensual bypath he pulled the covers up over his ears. He could have sworn he heard a voice from above reminding him of the Eleventh Commandment: *Thou shalt not covet thy golf partner's wife.*

11

At nine-forty in the morning Henry and Martha watched the jet from Milwaukee taxi up to disembark its passengers at Gate 44. As inconspicuously as possible he straightened his tie, smoothed his hair and adjusted his glasses. But because of morning fatigue he waited to square his shoulders and pull in his stomach until Janet and Bob Dunstan had made their appearance.

But only Bob arrived. Janet, he informed them, had just last night come down with the flu. Bob said he would have phoned about it but up until plane time both he and Janet had kept hoping she could make it. Perhaps, thought a disappointed Henry to himself, her absence was a blessing in disguise – he could not have focused his entire attention on playing in the Roundup tournament.

Two hours later he stood on the first tee of the two-day tournament, his heart pumping fast at the prospect of his initial drive. In that it was team low-ball medal play with full handicap, and in that Henry's handicap still stood at sixteen, despite his recent improved play, he sensed an excitement at the prospect that he and Bob Dunstan might solidly compete with the forty-five other teams. When Bob Dunstan commented on how fluid and strong Henry's practice swing appeared, Henry could not help but swell with pride.

'We'll get 'em, Bob,' he said, his voice ringing with surprising conviction. *My God*, thought Henry, *I've become a positive thinker!* And when his tee shot ended up as far down the first fairway as that of long-hitting Bob Dunstan or of either of their opponents, Henry felt at last he had matured as a competitive golfer.

With each subsequent shot his self confidence edged itself up another notch. His muscles had never before worked so well together, and his brain had the wisdom not to intrude with a lecture on how he should swing the club. After six holes of striking the ball with firm crispness, he found himself only two over par. On the seventh hole he curled in a twenty-foot downhill putt for a birdie. As the ball dropped from sight he clenched his fist and, in the manner of Tiger Woods, delivered a chopping macho uppercut into the air. God, what fun!

He soon realized his excitement had been premature. On three subsequent occasions he found himself in a bunker. Each time his mutinous inner voice rose up to haunt him. *You thought you were rid of me, eh Henry? Maybe you've outwitted me with your miracle ball and your tiny putter, but once you get in a sand trap, you're still my pigeon. OK, so you've promised yourself you're going to stay down to the ball and swing slowly. But that's not how it's gonna happen, sonny. You're gonna jump at it . . . .*

On all of those trips to hell in the sand he had bungled his shot miserably attacking the ball with his club as if trying to decapitate a snake. Although he double-bogeyed each of those holes, Bob Dunstan fortunately parred them.

When the first day scores were posted Henry and Bob stood only two shots off the lead. Henry, with his high handicap, had accounted for most of their net birdies but Bob's pars on the holes that Henry double-bogeyed had kept them from slipping down into the pack. Even so, Bob Dunstan seemed strangely unenthused – not his usual jovial self at all. Was he jealous of Henry's matching drives and more deadly putts? Or, God forbid! did Bob possess extra-sensory perception that had allowed him to tune in on Henry's last night's day-dream about his wife Janet?

Instead of celebrating his round with a few scotches, Henry promptly sought out club pro Jeff Logan. Together they spent a full hour in the practice sand-trap until Henry was confidently lobbing most of his shots to within a respectable distance of the pin. And his evil inner voice finally sneaked away with its tail between its legs.

On the second and final day of the tournament Bob Dunstan, with fire in his eyes, blistered the course with an incredible seventy. And perhaps by osmosis Henry found himself on the eighteenth green with a chance to break eighty for the first time in his life. With the green lined with spectators, Henry assumed his awkward crouch over his dwarf putter, then watched his putt trickle mercifully into the hole, assuring them of victory in the Rolling Hills Roundup.

In the true manner of a golfing champion letting off steam, and with just a hint of embarrassment, he hurled his golf cap high in the air as a souvenir for some lucky hero-worshipper in the crowd. To his surprise the only claimant was a Labrador retriever who quickly disappeared from sight with it.

Henry had no way of anticipating the far greater surprise that lay in wait that very evening.

Two hours later Henry put Bob Dunstan on a plane back to Milwaukee to keep an appointment with his lawyer first thing in the morning. The reason Janet had not accompanied him to the Roundup, Bob confessed upon leaving, was not because she had the flu at all. He had simply so advised the

Summerfills to avoid embarrassment all around. The truth was that he and Janet had just decided on a quickie divorce the following week. Henry felt bad indeed as he helped Bob carry his newly won tournament prize to the plane. But he didn't have time to dwell on Bob's problems for long – his own audience was waiting at the Roundup dinner dance.

As soon as he appeared on the scene Henry was hailed like a king, a position of eminence he had dreamed of so often but had never expected to attain. Even the younger wives – the ones with the flashing legs and the supple torsos whom previously he had only been able to observe from afar – now rushed forward to chat. Martha merely looked on, stupefied. And when amid great ceremony he was presented with the Roundup trophy as well as an imported $520 genuine Italian leather golf bag as first prize, Henry acknowledged the plaudits of the crowd with the most authentic man-of-the-people smile he could muster. He was determined to remain forever a modest, Tom Cruise sort of hero even though God had willed him to be a somewhat shorter version. But with each succeeding drink he began feeling taller.

'God Almighty,' man!' cried Alex Wulf, trapping him by the bar. 'What's come over you? I mean, this sort of thing just doesn't happen in golf. How do you account for being such a lousy chickenshit golfer a month ago and now, Jesus, this?' Then Alex laughed aloud. 'Hell, little buddy, can't you see I'm just jealous? Who wouldn't be jealous of someone you've beaten all your life who suddenly starts shooting pro-calibre golf?'

Henry let the words swirl deliciously inside his brain. 'Pro-calibre golf,' he whispered aloud. 'Do you really mean that, Alex?'

'Well, a seventy-nine isn't to be sneezed at. Even a top pro can't do that good sometimes.'

Henry gave vent to a long and wistful sigh. 'Wouldn't that be something just to play in one of those pro tournaments! Maybe even be on TV?'

The spark of an idea lit Alex's face. He gazed thoughtfully into his glass, then moved closer to utter a message of tantamount significance. 'Listen, Henry. I've got a fabulous idea as to how you might – just *might*, mind you – get your wish. How would you like to compete in a really major tournament?'

Henry eyed Alex with suspicion. 'What do you mean?'

'I mean nothing less than the granddaddy of them all, the greatest golf event in the world – the United States Open.'

'Dammit, Alex, just cut it out.'

'Hear me out, baby.' Alex Wulf swirled the ice cubes in his drink, his expression seeming to sober. 'Every tournament on the tour, except two, is sewed up by the pros, lock stock and barrel. If you're not a PGA pro you're not even allowed to try to qualify. The two exceptions are the Masters and the US Open. At the Masters you've got to be invited. And each year they ask eight or ten amateurs to compete. But hell, unless you've come in at the top of the heap in the National Amateur or some such, they don't even know your name, and couldn't care less. But the US Open, which is run by the United States Golf Association rather than by the PGA, is a horse of a different colour. All in all, they select a field of one hundred and fifty players. The only ones exempt from qualifying are the tournament winners and the very top money-makers of the previous year. That means they've got more than one hundred spots to be filled and they do it in the most democratic way possible. They conduct local qualifying rounds, open to pros and amateurs alike, in major communities all over the nation. Like maybe four thousand guys are trying out. The top half-dozen or so from each of those locals go on to compete in regional qualifying tournaments. And the top one hundred and twenty out of all those regionals get to compete in the US Open. Most of the qualifiers are pros, of course, because even a lot of the big-name touring pros have to go through that qualifying process just like anybody else. I read somewhere that last year only twelve amateurs in the country played well enough to get to the Open. It's a tough row to hoe, Henry, but, hell, why not give it a try? If you can keep improving at the pace you're going, think how much better you might be in another three weeks when the local qualifying rounds are held.'

Henry had remained silent out of courtesy. What Alex Wulf had recited had already found a place in Henry's own storehouse of golfing knowledge. Actually, Henry felt he knew one more extremely relevant fact about trying to qualify for the Open that Alex had apparently overlooked altogether.

'Maybe you're forgetting,' said Henry, 'that not just any amateur can even *enter* the local qualifying. The USGA says he's got to have a posted handicap of two or under. That lets me out by fourteen strokes.'

Alex was unimpressed with Henry's statement. 'Despite your academic study of the subject, Henry, there's more than one way to skin a cat. Bullshit on having to have a two handicap or better. That's not a hard and fast rule at all – it's just a guideline in case there are too many applicants for any particular local qualifying event. On the basis of your recent dramatically improved play, don't bet that I can't get you in.'

Henry experienced a sudden tingle at the tips of his ears. Could Alex possibly be on the level? When at last Henry spoke his voice was unable to disguise its trembling.

'Wh-what's your plan?'

Alex pointed to a tall, slightly tipsy stranger on the far side of the bar. 'Know him?' When Henry acknowledged that he didn't, Alex identified the man as Jackson Johns. 'He's the temporary USGA representative in charge of next month's local qualifying. He told me just tonight that they want a full field of guys trying to make it, but right now there don't seem to be that many pros and low-handicap amateurs around. Jackson was standing by the eighteenth green looking as impressed as hell when you finished up with that clutch putt. After he's had a few more drinks, just let me talk to him about you, OK?'

With reality fast closing in, Henry began to feel uneasy. It was one thing to compete in a friendly club tournament like the Rolling Hills Roundup but it was quite another thing to declare oneself a qualifying contestant for the US Open, particularly when one was surreptitiously playing with a doctored golf ball. But before Henry could politely decline his friend's offer, Alex pulled one more tempting surprise from his sleeve.

'Jackson told me not more than a half-hour ago that the local qualifying is not going to be played at Cedarcroft like it was planned. Some sort of beetle has chewed up their greens. It's been moved right here to Rolling Hills. Our course is a stranger to almost everyone who'll be trying to qualify. But not to you, Henry. You know every blade of grass on every green like the back of your hand. You know where all the trouble is, and you know the distance of every conceivable shot. That's gotta mean a four- or five-stroke advantage for you, right?'

Could it be that Alex was neither drunk nor completely out of his mind? When Henry felt his legs grow wobbly he wondered whether it was from having over-celebrated his Roundup victory or simply from the shock of what Alex was proposing. He grabbed another drink off the tray of a passing waiter and tried to concentrate on Alex's argument.

'Look, Henry, you owe it to your buddies to give it a try. We need *one* hero among us to add status to our whole group. And you've gotta be the guy. Who knows, you might have one helluva hot day at the local qualifying. You might just go on to the regional and have one helluva hot day there. If so, you're gonna find yourself competing, goddamnit, in the United States Open itself.' Alex's eyes, despite a touch of bleariness, kept blinking more brightly. 'You'd be the Cinderella Man of the golfing world. Say goodbye to Arnie's Army; here comes Henry's Henchmen ten thousand strong! How does that grab you?' Alex lowered his voice and moved closer to Henry's ear. 'What's more, hot-shot golfers attract pussy like catnip.'

Henry felt his cheeks growing warmer as he glanced away from the bar to make sure Martha had not suddenly material-ized from across the room.

'Just remember,' Alex was saying, 'every super success story in life has been written by a man who defied the odds.'

When in another five minutes Jackson Johns fumbled for an official entry form and Alex Wulf pulled out a pen, Henry had to steady his right wrist with his left hand in order to sign his name with any degree of legibility.

On the way home from the party he drove several blocks in silence. At last he reached for Martha's hand. When she moved closer, he felt the time was right to break out the big news.

'This may sound ridiculous – and I guess it really is – but I've been selected as a contestant in the local qualifying for the US Open.'

'Oh, wonderful, dear! Does that take place before or after our trip?'

'Our trip?'

'To Europe, Henry . . . . *Honestly!*'

69

After a quick and nervous calculation, he was pleased to state that the local qualifying was scheduled for five days prior to their intended departure. When Martha sighed with relief, Henry saw no reason to further mention that the regional qualifying in Milwaukee would take place *after* their departure date. But realistically that was hardly a factor.

12

The next morning Henry stared back at himself in the bathroom mirror. Despite his head feeling unusually heavy from too much partying, a smile still creased his face. But the longer he gazed at his reflection the more his smile began to fade. Wasn't his appearance at odds with how a truly competitive golfer was expected to look! Yes, something was definitely lacking. Could it by chance be the full head of hair he had owned as a teenager? Was there some way, he wondered, for him to fertilize his scalp, as Martha fertilized her garden, to cause a sudden profusion of growth? At least he could upgrade his image by letting his hair grow longer to allow him greater latitude in styling it in a more youthful and casual manner. Even Martha would be hard-pressed to create a pleasant flower arrangement if all she had to work with were a few scrawny chrysanthemum stems.

Nor would a more abundant yield of hair alone solve all his tonsorial problems. What could be more demoralizing than to compete against a field of fuzzy-cheeked youngsters who were years away from a single grey hair. Perhaps later in the day he should escape to the drugstore for a bottle of Grecian Formula. Just as in the television commercial he would kiss the grey goodbye so gradually over the course of the next several days that even his best friends would be none the wiser.

And as long as he planned to turn back the clock on top of his head, perhaps he should seek to improve other aspects of his image as well. His golf attire, for instance. How could he expect to win the admiration of others in non-colour-coordinated attire? The two were no more compatible than if an exotic dancer performed her act in a tailored skirt and shoulder bag. Although he certainly wouldn't become so extravagant as to outfit himself in the manner of Payne Stewart, at least he would begin wriggling out of his drab cocoon of nondescript golfing wear. And that, of course, led to further conjecture as to the appropriateness of his business clothes. Why play the role of Dr Jekyll and Mr Hyde? If for no other reason than the psychological boost it would give him, he'd make it a point also to sharpen up his downtown appearance even though his hours at the office seemed to be growing embarrassingly shorter.

Again he inspected his smile in the mirror. Yes, he would make a dental appointment as soon as possible. And while he was having his teeth cleaned, would it be displaying undue vanity to inquire about capping those two front incisors that failed to line up quite as perfectly as Robert Redford's?

'Thanks, Daddy,' said Katie a few evenings later. She carefully counted out the roll of notes he handed her, then delivered three more modified Top-Flites to her father. 'That makes an even dozen so far,' she said. 'Will you be needing more?'

'Oh, but definitely, honey. I use a new ball every few rounds. As you mentioned some time ago, their special properties gradually seem to give out a bit.'

Katie nodded. 'All that pounding with the club finally begins to alter their induced molecular arrangement.' She looked above and beyond him. 'Golly, that might also affect the qualitative calibration of my display proof for the science fair . . . . Let's see, if I . . . .'

'Katie,' he interrupted, 'here are another dozen Top-Flites for you to work with. Could you have at least some of them ready by the weekend? I'm practising almost every afternoon, you know, and that tends to deplete my supply faster.'

'How much do you think I should charge you, Daddy?'

He stared back at her, surprised. 'The going rate has been twenty dollars a ball, Katie.'

'For the first dozen, yes. We agreed to renegotiate after that, remember? And I've just delivered the last of those first twelve.'

Henry shifted from one foot to the other, then pointed out that in the normal course of business most suppliers extend a discount on wholesale orders.

His daughter remained unimpressed. 'The new price,' she said, 'will be forty dollars a ball.'

'Katie! You're money mad!'

'Not at all, Daddy. It's not the money I want – it's the new computerized equipment I can buy with it. Anyway, I shouldn't really take the time just now. The science fair is only a week away and . . . .'

Henry was more interested in the here and now. 'How about thirty dollars?'

She gazed into his face, a slow, reproving smile forming on her lips. 'Answer me one question, Daddy. Since you started playing with these new balls, have you paid more for my services than you've won on the golf course?'

Henry gazed at the floor of his daughter's laboratory, unable to meet her glance. 'All right,' he said at last. 'Forty dollars a ball it is.'

'Plus,' added Katie, 'a special one-time non-cash bonus.'

'A bonus? Like what?'

'A pair of contact lenses.' She removed her thick-lensed glasses with a frown. 'It's just that these keep distorting things under a microscope. I can't get my eye down over the viewfinder well enough.' When she put them back on she studied her father's appearance. 'Maybe you should get some contacts too,' she said. 'Those glasses of yours are even more out of fashion than mine. They don't go at all with those new tartan trews you're wearing. And, golly, you're letting your hair grow, aren't you?' She circled him observantly. 'Is this just a deceptive light, Daddy, or are you also dyeing it?'

Henry cast his daughter a sheepish grin. 'I guess I'm self-conscious about, you know, how I'll look to all those young golfers when I tee up at the qualifying round.'

'Neat, Daddy. That's the old spirit.'

Again he dropped his eyes, only absently noting his new casual loafers.

'You're not just putting me on, are you, Katie? I mean, do you *really* think I'd look better in contacts?'

Henry sat on the floor of his den, nude to the waist, facing his newly purchased sun-lamp. Feeling strong was a state of mind as well as of muscle. And who could deny that a bronzed complexion didn't go a long way towards convincing even the sickliest of mortals that he was more stalwart than if his pallor resembled that of a monastery monk? Right now, with the thirty-six-hole local qualifying event only five days away, Henry needed all the physical, mental and divine help he could rally. Especially considering his last two disappointing rounds of golf.

While his game in general had kept on track since winning the Rolling Hills Roundup, his new stubby putter had recently turned saboteur. An even higher percentage of his short putts were missing the hole. As a consequence his confidence had begun dropping as fast as last year's junk bonds with the result that he felt more bearish each time he stooped over to putt. He feared that the ball wasn't going to drop in the hole. And it didn't. To make matters worse there was nothing he could do to try to remedy his deficient putting with practice. He had learned painfully from experience that such prolonged and repetitive crouching was a sure way of sending him to bed for a week with his spinal cord tied in a knot.

With another five minutes to go in front of the sun-lamp, Henry resumed his isometric exercises, cupping the fingers of his left hand with the fingers of his right. For six seconds he tugged one against the other with all his strength, repeating the exercise five times. When he finished, he felt his forearms to see whether that important set of golfing muscles had developed further in the past week. If so, perhaps he could add another few yards to his tee shots. But what good would that do if he couldn't pull out of his putting slump? Perhaps what he needed most was an attitude adjustment. Slowly then and with profound deliberation Henry lifted his chin towards the sun-lamp as if he were a marine facing the American flag. In addition to the ultraviolet rays seeping into his skin he imagined a monstrous dose of positivism flooding through every pore of his body.

You'll putt like a demon, Henry Summerfill! He kept repeating those words over and over again, trying hard to programme them with everlasting performance into the putting control-centre of his brain. But his invaluable spell of self-hypnosis was shattered when he heard Martha call his name. As her voice grew nearer he snapped off his sun-lamp, grabbed a magazine and plopped himself in a chair. 'Yes dear,' he called. 'I'm here in the den.'

'Henry,' she said, arriving on the scene. 'I know I've asked you this before but I just want to make sure your golfing plans aren't going to keep us from going to Europe.'

'Sure we're going.'

'But what if you should make it to the regional, or whatever you call it? That won't be played till two-days after the garden-club charter flight leaves.'

'Look, Martha, let's be realistic. The local qualifying is next Monday. I'm only competing because, well, I let Alex Wulf talk me into it. I just want to play well enough not to make an ass of myself. There's no way for me to go on to the regional.'

'How can I be sure of that! This past month has been so absolutely crazy. One day you tell me you're giving up golf for good and then you turn around and spend every waking minute on the course. Do you go to the office at all any more?'

'Actually, Martha, my income this month happens to be up quite a bit.' Henry saw no reason to confuse his wife by advising her how much had been from his business activities as opposed to how much had been earned on the golf course.

'Well,' she said, 'if you're sure we're still going, don't you think you should have your passport picture retaken?'

'But I just had it taken last month.'

She held out his passport. 'I'm not sure you'd be allowed to leave the States with this sort of identification, Henry. Your hair is a different shape and colour. Your teeth are capped. You've developed a deep tan. And you don't wear glasses any more.'

'I wear contacts, Martha. To my knowledge there's nothing in international law that says a near-sighted person has to fly the Atlantic in old-fashioned spectacles.'

She laughed then and kissed the top of his head. 'Just teasing, dear,' she said, leaving the room.

Henry wondered why she was behaving more strangely

with each passing week. He shrugged then, smiling with benevolence in the masculine solitude of his den . . . . Ah women! Who could ever hope to understand them!

Before retiring to bed, in keeping with his recently inaugurated policy of promoting a healthy body inside and out, he downed double his twice-a-day ration of vitamins A, B, C, D and E. During next Monday's local qualifying event every little hormone in his body would need to perform at peak efficiency to help him get round those thirty-six holes.

13

At 8.30 on Monday morning – the exact time that Henry normally reported for work at the office – he paced nervously beside the first tee of the Rolling Hills Country Club awaiting the starter's call. The official local qualifying for the United States Open had already begun, and only six men from a field of 141 area pros and top amateurs would earn the right to go on to the regional. When Henry realized that within the next ten minutes he would begin his arduous thirty-six-hole trek he immediately ceased his pacing and sat down on a bench. Unfortunately, a pre-tournament jogging resolution to strengthen his legs had not materialized as he had planned. On his first outing a surly Rottweiler had denied him free access to the footpath, informing Henry in so many growls that he would dispose of him completely if he had the gall to pass that way again. Apparently some irresponsible canine had spread the rumour that Henry Summerfill had imported the flea to America. Rather than taking a chance on extensive physical damage to his person, Henry had stowed his jogging gear away in a cupboard, concluding that two less-than-strong legs were better than none at all.

Today, unfortunately, his legs were more out of shape than usual. The science fair had gone on all weekend in the downtown cement-floored venue where he and Martha had helped their daughter set up and dismantle her complex display. And because Katie had seemed so small and alone in the midst of that milling throng they had remained with her, fetching her an occasional soft drink and making the rounds of hundreds of other displays to report back to her – no doubt ineptly but as best they could – on what they had seen. And when for the third straight year she captured first prize, including a cheque for $400, Henry hugged his daughter so tightly that he all but squeezed the breath out of them both.

'Thanks for everything,' she said as they drove home. 'I feel guilty, Daddy, that you skipped golf just for me. Especially with your big day coming up tomorrow.'

'I'm better off not having practised anyway, Katie. Football teams take it easy before a game. That's what I've been doing here with you – just trying to forget it so I won't be so nervous at tee-off time.'

Once they were home, Katie took her father aside.

'Maybe I shouldn't even mention this,' she said at last, 'but my usual procedure in treating your golf balls got a little crossed up on that batch I delivered you the night before last.'

Henry felt himself shudder – he had not yet played with them and those were the only balls he had to play with in tomorrow's qualifying tournament.

'Wh-what do you mean, crossed up?'

'Now, Daddy, don't panic. It was just that Mom called me upstairs to pick up my clothes after I'd begun one of the more delicate steps.' Katie went on to explain that since the matter of the doctored balls still remained secret between her and her father, she could not fabricate any plausible excuse not to obey her mother's insistent demands. The result was that the Top-Flites were left for a longer period than usual while undergoing pulsations of electromagnetization.

'If they're different in any respect,' she concluded, 'it would be such a subtle change that it would hardly affect their playing properties at all .... Please stop looking so nervous, Daddy. I'm just sure they'll be all right.'

Now seated on the bench beside the first tee Henry reached into his hip pocket and pulled out the balls he would be playing with in today's tournament – his Katie-altered Top-Flite-3 for use for tee to green, and a regular Top-Flite-2 he would use for putting. He rolled his new miracle ball between his fingers, staring at its white dimpled contour in hopes that the ball itself might reassure him that it had no wicked new tricks up its sleeve.

He looked around at the other contestants in the vicinity, all youthful and flat-bellied and steely-nerved. Henry abstractedly touched a hand to his hair, now more luxuriant and darker than only a few weeks ago. He hoped that these youngsters looked upon him as more in the vintage of an older brother than a father. He stood up from the bench and turned his back as he attempted to adjust more comfortably the wide elastic abdominal supporter he was wearing beneath his emerald green shirt and his multicoloured slacks. While the supporter had a tendency to pinch his stomach, especially while he was seated, there was no doubt it sufficiently deflated his belly to warrant that slight bit of discomfort.

Henry jumped at the sound of a voice booming from a nearby loudspeaker ....

'On the tee – Beanie Broadhurst, Jeff Logan and Henry Summerfill.'

He rose, his mouth dry, his chest thumping mightily. At least he was grateful that Jeff Logan had made arrangements to be in his threesome. As they stepped to the tee, the club pro placed a shepherding hand on his member's shoulder.

'This isn't the end of the world, Henry. Just relax and enjoy it.'

A tall gangling youngster bounced across the tee to extend a monstrous hand.

'Hello, Mr Summerfill. I'm Beanie Broadhurst.'

'Just call me Henry ... or Hank, if you like.'

'Yes sir. I sure will, sir.'

Henry gaped in amazement at the sight of Jeff's and Beanie's drives soaring all but out of sight down the first fairway. When he then bent down to tee up his own ball his abdominal supporter pinched him sharply. He took his stance, checked the position of his feet and hands, said a quick prayer and swung the club. When his first shot of the day flew modestly down the fairway with only a slight banana fade he breathed a sigh of relief. At least he had not utterly disgraced himself. He set forth on foot down to the first of thirty-six holes with the feeling he was starting off on a safari to Kilimanjaro. The butterflies in his stomach began settling down when he discovered that his Top-Flite had rolled to a stop not too many yards short of the other two balls. He raised his eyes to the clear blue sky of May, peering through his soft contacts in search of his twelve-year-old daughter. *Thanks Katie. The ball's OK.*

Beanie Broadhurst was scratching his head in disbelief.

'My God, Mr Summerfill sir – I mean, Henry, sir – I've never seen so much overspin on a ball in all my life. I didn't think you'd get half this far. And you swung so easy!'

'Freddie Couples swings easy too,' Henry ventured.

'Hey, that's right. Well, I'll be damned.'

Soon after Henry lofted his approach to within twenty feet of the pin he realized the time had come to find out whether his recent putting slump was still with him. Just the thought of it reawakened the butterflies in his stomach. After lining up his putt he crouched down over his putting ball, his knuckles white on the handle of his dwarf putter. Despite his resolve to think positive, his mutinous inner voice returned to haunt him . . . . *You've got the yips, Henry. You're getting to that age, you know. Maybe you can fool yourself with your new youthful image and that flashy outfit you're wearing but you can't fool Mother Nature. And just look at how you're bent double over the ball with your butt higher than your head! No wonder your ears are ringing! Sure, I agree the green looks fast as hell but it's not gonna get any slower. Hurry up and putt, for chrissake, before you get a crick in your spine . . . .*

Henry three-putted the green.

And he three-putted the next, and the next, carding bogeys on the first three holes as opposed to the straight pars posted by Jeff Logan and young Broadhurst. He was walking up the fourth fairway, his head hung low, when Jeff edged over beside him.

'Perhaps you aren't aware of a certain USGA rule, Henry, because we don't enforce it in club membership play – and believe me, I'm not saying this to be critical – but you're not allowed to change balls during play on a hole. On the last green I noticed you used a different ball for putting.'

Henry turned to his pro in shocked surprise.

'My God, Jeff . . . . Should I disqualify myself?'

'Oh, hell no, Henry. I just know you want to abide by the rules of the game, that's all. Beginning now just remember to play out each hole with the ball you select for your tee shot. If Broadhurst noticed, he'd be within his rights in calling it on you.'

The more Henry thought about it as he neared the fourth green, the more he began to panic. For the remainder of the day he could either choose to play entire holes with the regular ball he used for putting but which he couldn't drive more than 180 yards, or instead he could start putting with his supercharged Top-Flite. And if he did that, what sort of insane performance might he exhibit on the greens? Three-putting was bad enough but if he began knocking putts from one fringe to the other as he had done some weeks ago when first trying out the ball – well, he hated to think what Jeff Logan might begin to suspect. On this hole, unfortunately, he had no choice. He had hit his recently modified miracle ball off the tee on this par-three hole to where it now rested on the green some thirty feet from the flag.

As he went through the motions of lining up his putt he knew that it sighted straight but he had no idea how gently to tap it. He paced from his ball to the hole and back again, pretending to study each blade of grass along the way, but, in fact, he knew he was only postponing the moment of truth. At last he crouched down into his awkward stance, his hands so shaky that he could hardly grip the putter. He took careful aim, sucked in his breath and tapped the ball even more weakly than he had planned. Worse still, he had felt himself pull it woefully off line. For what seemed for ever Henry kept his eyes glued to the spot where his ball had lain, refusing to face up to the anguish of watching his putt die half-way to the hole and far to the left.

When he finally raised his eyes he was astonished to find the ball still rolling steadily onwards – slowly, slowly, now beginning to curl counter to the slope of the green in a pronounced arc towards the hole. As Jeff Logan and Beanie Broadhurst watched in stunned silence, the ball plopped dead centre into the cup for Henry's first – but far from last – birdie of the day.

14

'I knew you could do it, Daddy. Oh, I'm so proud of you!' Katie leaped into his arms, laughing victoriously. Then she stepped back to study his face. 'You look so tired. Are you OK?'

Henry sank heavily on to the living-room sofa. 'I'm OK, other than that my legs have petrified.' He kicked off his loafers and lay back his head. 'Do me a big favour, sweetie, and fix me a martini.'

'How do I do that?'

'Put some ice cubes in a tall glass and fill it with vodka . . . . Where's your mother?'

'At some travel lecture on Italy. She went with a couple of ladies who are taking the same trip as yours.'

Henry was too exhausted to face up to the fact that the impossible had happened – his forthcoming golf schedule and Martha's overseas itinerary were headed on a collision course. How could he have suspected his astounding putting would propel him onwards and upwards to the regional qualifying at Milwaukee two weeks hence? After the first healthy swallow of his drink his corpuscles began to stir. I just don't understand how it happened, he heard himself mutter.

'Tell me about it, Daddy. I take it that what I did differently to those new Top-Flites didn't really matter.'

For some time Henry studied his stockinged feet.

'I think it mattered a great deal,' he said finally. He told her of his initial panic when Jeff Logan had advised him he would have to putt the ball he'd teed off with. 'Believe me, honey, all I had to do was just get my putts started in the general direction of the hole. It got to be downright embarrassing how often they dropped in. Tell me, what could have made the ball behave like that?'

Katie silently contemplated the matter, then shrugged.

'Maybe you've just become the world's most skilful putter.'

'I'd like to believe that but I can't. I could tell I wasn't stroking the ball well at all. Sometimes I was positive my putt would stop short or, at other times, that it would run well past the hole. Or maybe I'd feel myself jerking the putt to the left or pushing it out to the right. But so often even that didn't seem to make any difference. It was as if the hole was a magnet.'

'A magnet, hummm?' Katie lowered her eyes, seeming to float off in a trance. Henry could all but feel her alpha waves bounce back at him from the living-room walls. 'What are greens made of?' she asked finally. 'I mean, what's the top-soil like just under the grass?'

'I've never thought about it . . . . Oh, now wait a minute. I haven't read it but this last issue of *Golf* magazine has an article on the composition of greens. It's right there on the coffee table.' He had no sooner spoken than Martha stepped through the front door.

'Henry,' she said. 'You survived!'

'He not only survived, Mom, he's going on to compete in the regional.'

Henry dropped his glance and slowly sipped his drink. When the prolonged silence got to him, he ever-so-gradually lifted his eyes to find Martha looking into his face. Finally, her non-committal expression gave way to a smile compounded of both forgiveness and pride.

'Congratulations, dear,' she said. 'I hope all your dreams come true.' She bent down to pat his arm, then helped him to his feet. 'Be a good boy, Henry, and go take a hot bath. Then we'll have to talk.'

Long after dark that same night Henry reclined on the patio *chaise-longue* in his robe and slippers, now and then trying to rub the soreness from his legs as he sought to explore his conscience. No one was present to distract him. Katie was in her room while Martha kept busy on the phone making new arrangements for the European trip. She had decided to tour the Continent with two of her garden-club friends whose husbands had to drop out of the charter flight because of last-minute business entanglements. But Henry had dropped out because of golf, and that made him feel guilty. Earlier in the day he had beaten Beanie Broadhurst out of a qualifying berth in the regional and *that* made him feel guilty. And because the regional was to be played in Milwaukee, that made him feel guiltiest because that was where newly-divorced Janet Dunstan now lived all alone. The voice of his conscience began prodding him to write to Jackson Johns to say that he had been called to attend an emergency session of the International Securities Analysts Council in Paris and, regretfully, would be unable to compete in the regional qualifying tournament.

'Daddy, is that you sitting in the dark?'

'Yes, Katie, hi.'

'May I join you?'

'Of course.'

She pulled up a patio chair next to his *chaise-longue*.

'I read the magazine article on the composition of greens, Daddy, and I've been giving that question of yours a lot of study. I think I've figured out why your new Top-Flite worked such magic when you were putting today.'

For the next quarter of an hour she talked without stopping, beginning her discourse in such simple layman's language that Henry followed her thoughts completely. But after her first pause for breath Henry started losing his way until, at the end, he might as well have been listening to an opera sung in German.

Under the grass on greens, she had begun, was a top-soil layer of up to eighty-five per cent sand with just enough mixture of peat moss and soil to hold it together without shifting. That was why greens drained so quickly and well. But the real guts of what she was about to propound centred on the sand itself, composed as it was of tiny mineral and rock particles.

'By far the most common denominator found in sand – and here's the key, Daddy – is quartz. So where does that lead us? Well it leads us back to 1880 and Pierre Curie's discovery of the piezo-electric effect. As you probably know, that's the unusual property of adjacent quartz surfaces which when squeezed together develop positive and negative electric charges vibrating at a natural frequency. Now let's move on to how that could influence your putting with any of those last three Top-Flites I processed. You told me the greens were fast which I presume means the grass was cut shorter, making for less insulation than normal between your ball and the compacted sandy soil. Are you with me?'

'Keep going.' Henry was no longer reclining – he had scooted himself to the edge of the *chaise-longue* to grasp more readily what his daughter might be leading up to.

'By means of theoretical trial and error I discarded the

possibility of silicon interaction, of supersonic inversion and of spectra-fluorescent bombardment. Then, just out of the blue, it came to me – oscillatory rejection. In plainer words, Daddy, a ball subjected to excessive electronmagnetization, as happened with these last three Top-Flites, responds with a degree of negativity to those minuscule frequency vibrations in the compacted quartz sand. In effect, the ball seeks the absence of such impulses. And there's only one spot on the green that is free from them – the hole itself! Getting back to what I said a moment ago, the shorter the grass, the more pronounced the reaction of the ball in seeking the hole. It's as simple as that.'

'Amazing!' Henry barely whispered the word as he rose to his feet. As if hypnotized he stepped from the patio into the garden, all the while gazing into the firmament. '*Amazing!*' he breathed again. But the longer he dwelled on this miracle his daughter had wrought, the more he found himself losing a battle with his conscience.

Henry turned in the darkness to find his daughter at his elbow. 'I just can't go through with it,' he heard himself say. 'I've never intentionally broken a law in my life and I'm not going to keep on violating the rules of the United States Golf Association. It's just about the last rampart of decency in the whole world. I'm going to disqualify myself from competing in the regional.'

They stood together under the stars, not speaking as her hand slipped into his.

'Daddy,' she said finally, 'listen to me.'

She then told him that while she had been reading *Golfing* magazine her curiosity had been piqued by what she had found in so many other pages. She had discovered both in editorial content and in ads that the entire golfing industry, as well as the top players of the game, were constantly searching for ways to improve the performance of both clubs and balls.

'First there were wood-shafted clubs,' she said. 'Then they began making shafts out of steel and of fibreglass and of aluminium and of graphite. And now heads of titanium. Irons are now both forged and cast. Some have concave soles, some have bevelled soles; some have pear-shaped heels, some have offset hosels, whatever that means; some have cavity backs and others have tungsten inserts. And, yes, Daddy, the same sort of experimenting goes on with golf balls, too. They keep modifying the size and shape of the dimples for improved aerodynamics and they fool around with balata and Surlyn, and they try solid centres and tumble-frozen liquid centres tucked inside computerized high-speed windings.'

Katie paused to catch her breath, then looked up at him. 'If all those things don't add up to horsing around with golfing equipment, I don't know what does. It's just that you and I may have been luckier in finding a better way to accomplish what everyone else is so frantic to discover. What's more, we've not violated a single USGA specification as to a ball's size or weight. Nor have we even modified its allowable initial velocity.'

Henry lifted his eyes to the night – his daughter had just sent his spirits soaring. At the same time she had freed his conscience. An army of Roto-Rooter men could not have drained away his guilt more effectively. He had no excuse left for not carrying on. If there was any real manhood about him at all, he just couldn't let his daughter down. Nor his golfing buddies. Nor, more significantly, himself. An unexpected tremor of courage began seeping upwards from the damp midnight earth through the soles of his slippers. Slowly but surely it gained momentum, flowing upwards past his bone-weary legs till it all but gorged his heart. Suddenly he clutched Katie tightly against him, rocking her to and fro.

'It's you and me against the world, my little sweetie genius. Onwards and upwards to glory!'

Under the placid starry sky Henry Summerfill was so transfixed by the recitation of that indomitable vow that he failed to hear the rumble of thunder just over the horizon of his tomorrow's world.

15

After holing out the final putt of his morning round at the regional in Milwaukee Henry would have liked nothing better than to find a hot bath in the Canterbury Club-house to soak away his stress before his final eighteen holes of the day.

In the past he had thought his customary weekend foursome battles at Rolling Hills to be stressful enough. But that stress multiplied itself at the member-guest Roundup tournament, then multiplied again at the local qualifying for the US Open. Now at the regional his stress level was fast reaching the point of no return. Even his phenomenal putting, for which he could take but slight credit, failed to compensate for his errant drives and miscalculated iron-play. As a result, after reviewing the posted scores of all sixty-four contestants, he found himself far back in the pack. In his mind already he could hear the fat lady sing – there was no way he could catch up enough to capture one of the six top spots that would propel those players into the United States Open in Denver.

So as not to delay tee-off times for the afternoon round a buffet table had been set up with sandwiches, chicken salad, pickles and a choice of soft drinks. Henry glanced at his watch while he waited in line, dismayed to find that less than thirty minutes remained until his threesome had to embark upon that same four-mile trek all over again.

After he had filled his plate he glanced around for someone as company. But all the others were clustered in groups. Even his two playing mates, Chico Alvarez and Al Blenheim, had gone to join a huddle in a far corner. Henry took a step in that direction but paused when the group exploded in laughter. Was their mirth provoked by a joke, Henry wondered, or by the insensitive Chico informing the others about Henry's ridiculous putting posture? Henry turned and carried his plate down the long back hallway to a remote and deserted bench in the locker room.

When he bit into his sandwich his taste buds savoured it no more than his stomach seemed in the mood to digest it. He scooped up a forkful of chicken salad, lifted it to his lips, then put it down without a bite. Somehow he wasn't hungry. He put his plate aside, pushed the butt end of the bench against the wall, laid his back upon it and raised his legs, resting his feet against the wall at a nearly ninety-degree angle from his body. Ah, that would help! As he felt the pressure ease, first from his feet and then from his aching calves, he closed his eyes. Yes, his presence here at the regional against such stiff competition seemed incongruous indeed. He was, after all, only an obscure out-of-condition investment analyst who rightfully should be hunched over his desk in the office or, more appropriately, taking snapshots of Martha in an Amsterdam tulip garden. When he had put her on that charter flight to Europe two days ago he had been struck with such a feeling of remorse for not accompanying her that he had vowed to refrain from contacting Janet Dunstan while here in her home town. But fate, it seemed, had been determined to shatter his resistance. As he waited in the airport for his flight here to Milwaukee he had stepped over to a bookstand to see if the new *Golf Digest* was there. But a provocatively-titled bestseller caught his eye first. He glanced both right and left, then quickly picked it up to glance at a random page.

Many authorities have come to doubt that the majority of men and women are happiest when monogamous and faithful. It may be that many who remain faithful to a single partner throughout life pay dearly in terms of frustration, resentment of their mates, desiccation of their emotions, and the limitation of their potential for rich and rewarding lives . . . .

Henry had forced himself to replace the book in a hurry and proceed to his airport gate. Those words had simply underscored what Alex Wulf had preached just last week. *You know what a nut you've become about keeping in shape, Henry. Well, have you read about the physical benefits of sex to men past forty? Every piece of tail is equivalent to an hour of jogging. Better yet, it firms up your back, helps flatten your gut and strengthens your heart. You'll actually live longer with some adulterous adventures along the line.*

Last night, dining alone in a Milwaukee restaurant, Henry had unfolded a piece of paper from his pocket, stared at a number, then recklessly hurried to a phone booth. He dropped in his coin, dialled the first few digits, paused a moment, then slowly replaced the instrument in its cradle. He walked back to his table, alone and lonely but with his virtue still intact.

Now lying on the locker-room bench in the Canterbury Country Club he was surprised to realize how much he missed Martha. And that evening he would be flying home, freed from the temptation of proposing a rendezvous with Janet Dunstan.

93

But why was he letting his mind wander like this? His immediate concern was finding the energy to negotiate these forthcoming final eighteen holes. After another five minutes of staring at his elevated feet he eased himself down into a sitting position on the bench, climbed back into his golf shoes and adjusted his elastic waistband for maximum possible comfort. He popped two 500 mg Stresstabs into his mouth and retraced his steps down the long back hallway to the snack bar where he purchased three chocolate bars for additional quick-energy at intervals during his afternoon round.

Two and a half hours later, after having consecutively bogeyed the ninth, tenth and eleventh holes he only wanted this golfing agony to come to an end. Even the pleasant Mrs Betty Budd, who accompanied the threesome as group scorer for the afternoon round, seemed silently to commiserate with his faltering efforts to keep pace with the par onslaughts of his two playing opponents.

But from the time Al Blenheim addressed his tee shot on the twelfth hole until Henry and Betty Budd arrived as a solitary duo at the fourteenth green, he could hardly believe what had happened all over the Canterbury golf course in that crazy half-hour. First it had been Al, then a golfer in the threesome ahead of them. Then Chico, then two contestants on an adjoining hole – each breaking out in a cold sweat before doubling up in contortions and commencing to vomit. Suddenly there were golf carts racing towards every hole on the course to return the afflicted to the clubhouse. From a distance Henry could hear sirens of approaching ambulances.

'My God! What's going on?' Henry asked Betty Budd.

'I'm not sure but are *you* all right, Mr Summerfill – I mean, Henry?'

'I – I think so,' he said. 'I'm pretty tired but that's nothing new.'

'What did you have for lunch?'

'Nothing,' he said. 'I didn't feel like eating.'

'Maybe that's been your salvation. Yours and all the caddies. Tell me, were they serving the golfers anything in particular?'

'They had a buffet,' said Henry, 'sandwiches, pickles, and some warmed-up chicken salad . . . .'

'Chicken salad!' Betty Budd's eyes lit up like those of Sherlock Holmes. 'There's your culprit.'

'I feel like I ought to be back at the club-house helping the victims,' said Henry after putting out on the fourteenth. 'Just look around. I'm practically the only golfer in sight.'

'Unless you keep a stomach-pump in your golf bag you'd only add to the confusion.' She recorded his bogey, then waved him towards the fifteenth tee. 'Don't worry,' she said. 'They'll all be good as new by morning.'

In another hour Henry stared dumbfounded at the scoreboard on the all but deserted club terrace. Opposite almost all of the contestants' names was emblazoned the word WITH-DREW . . . .

The longer he studied the scores, the more he began realizing that the aria he had heard earlier in the day was only in his imagination. Now the fat lady was singing for real, dedicating her clear, dulcet tones to Henry D. Summerfill who finished in sixth place to earn the last qualifying berth to the United States Open.

'Do you think we can make the airport in time?' Henry glanced out of the taxi window at the early-evening traffic. One thing was for sure – he couldn't get on the plane without first ducking quickly into the men's room. 'My flight takes off in another twenty-three minutes.'

'All I can do is try, pal. Why is it you guys always wait till the last minute to call a cab?'

Henry was tempted to explain that as a qualifier for the United States Open he had assented to a locker-room interview with a sportswriter from the *Milwaukee Sentinel*. But when he studied the taxi driver's identification picture posted in front of him, Henry concluded that the man wouldn't appreciate what he was talking about anyway. Realistically he had to admit that the story probably would not even appear. But on this particular day, if the world remained free from homicides, robberies, hijackings, tornadoes, earthquakes and breakdowns in international relations, perhaps there would be a paragraph or two tucked away in the sports section that he could send to Martha overseas.

When Henry again checked his wrist-watch he discovered he had but twelve minutes left till his plane was scheduled to depart. He shifted uncomfortably in the back seat, his bladder about to burst. 'Aren't we about there?'

'Five more minutes, pal. Believe me, I'm breakin' my goddamn neck to get you there on time.'

He sat back and tried to relax as the taxi's meter continued eating up his dollars as if it hadn't been fed for days.

'Here you are, pal. We made it just like I promised.'

In another moment Henry was racing with his suitcase and genuine Italian leather golf bag towards Gate 46 which, as he had feared, was located as far as possible from where the cabbie had set him down. When a clock in the terminal corridor indicated he had but two minutes left till flight time, he tried to move his weary legs even faster, but the only thing that accelerated its pace was his pulse. At last he was there and, yes, a few passengers still stood waiting in line to embark. Nothing could have been more fortuitous than for

Henry to spy a men's room not six paces from where he stood. He quickly ducked inside and released the dammed-up pressure from his abdominal wall. But in his haste to zip up his fly he ensnared his shirt-tail, jamming the zipper before it had hardly started on its uphill run. He yanked at it frantically to no avail, only wedging the shirt-tail tighter. At last, after calming himself enough to master the mechanical solution to his problem, he dashed from the men's room only to find that Gate 46 had clanked irrevocably shut – he had missed the last plane home until morning.

Henry turned away dismayed. What of the hours immediately ahead? Must he face another dreary dinner alone? Wasn't there someone with whom he could share this pinnacle moment in his golfing career? Who was he kidding – the answer was excitingly, frighteningly clear. Without taking time to talk himself out of it he hastily found a phone booth, unfolded the slip of paper from his pocket and dialled the number. He was scarcely able to hear the ringing of the phone above the pounding of his heart.

16

'I still can't believe what a happy coincidence this is,' Janet Dunstan slowly revolved the candle on the table between them. 'There I was about to come to the airport anyway and here you were holed up in this motel resigned to having a few drinks alone. I mean, it worked out perfectly, didn't it, Henry?'

'Yes,' he agreed, 'perfectly.' His eyes left hers only long enough to flag down their waitress for another round of drinks.

'Goodness, Henry, you'll have me drunk before I even start my trip. What will my sister think when she sees me being poured off the plane in Dallas?' Her laughter gave way to a teasing pout. 'Remember in college when you deserted me at the Junior Prom? I just couldn't believe that anyone as nice as you would stand me up that way.'

'I *didn't* stand you up. A fraternity brother got deathly ill from trying to chugalug a pint of gin. Someone had to drive him to the dispensary quick.'

'But he wasn't your date. *I* was. Really, Henry, what else was I to believe but that you'd chickened out on me?' She ran a finger up the cuff of his sleeve. 'But you're not a chicken any more, are you?' Before he could frame an answer she was getting to her feet. 'Excuse me a minute, darling. In my rush to meet you here I neglected to make a phonecall.'

Alone at the table Henry stared into his glass as if it were a crystal ball. Where, he wondered, were things headed now? Janet had no sooner answered his phonecall than she had volunteered she was catching a plane at 10.30 that night. Whether he had then suggested they should get together for these intervening few hours, or whether she had, he could not now remember. But here they were alone in the cocktail bar of the motel where he was lodged till morning. Random impressions of the past hour tumbled over one another in his mind . . . . He had still not had dinner and each martini was spinning his head faster . . . . Janet Dunstan seemed infinitely more beguiling now than as a coed, and she kept implying the same about him . . . . She had cheered his golfing exploits and he had sympathized with her recently-terminated marital woes . . . . It seemed that her eyes had been delving more deeply into his as the minutes kept passing and their drinks kept emptying . . . . And less than a minute ago she had called him *darling*. Was it only of the Zsa Zsa Gabor type, he wondered, or, rather, fraught with deeper undercurrents? If it was the latter, what was expected of him in return? In any event her plane was due to depart in another hour and a half.

While he waited for Janet's return he envisaged how things might materialize if they moved on to his room . . . . *Oh, Henry darling, that feels so good . . . . Where in the world did you learn? – I mean, oh Lord, I never knew it could be this way – never ever knew, never ever knew, oooo . . . .*

But then the scales of Henry's reasoning teetered from unlikely *pro* to far more likely *con* . . . . *Go to your room? Really, Henry, what led you to believe I'd agree to anything like that? We've been having fun just visiting, haven't we? Or have you grown too callous to give a damn about renewing friendships for the sake of friendship alone? . . . . No, I won't accept your apology, I mean, it's all so sordid and dirty . . . . Oh, your poor dear Martha . . . .*

Janet returned, hoisted her drink and cast him a slow smile. 'What are you thinking?' she asked.

'Who, me? Nothing – nothing at all.'

'Then why do you keep breaking those plastic swizzle sticks into smaller and smaller pieces? Are you concerned about our being alone together?'

'No ... uh, no, of course not.'

She sipped her drink and slowly lifted her eyes. 'You know something, Henry – you're sexy. I can tell that behind that shy smile of yours beats the heart of a devil.'

Henry felt himself grow warm under the collar. 'You're teasing me, Janet.'

She reached for his hand just loosely enough for her fingertips to tickle his palm. 'Darling, I was never more serious in my life.'

At last Henry knew what was expected of him. But his voice seemed more like that of a stranger when he spoke.

'What would you think of finishing our drinks in, uh, my room?'

Janet surprised him by laughing aloud. 'Dear God in Heaven, I thought you'd never ask!'

He followed her down the outside walkway towards his room, noticing the sway of her hips. His mouth grew dry and a knot tightened in his stomach . . . . *Relax, old boy. Every man needs this sort of thing. Remember what Alex Wulf told you? – it's physical conditioning at its best and you've got to be in top shape for the Open.*

After reaching for his room key he hoped Janet didn't notice that his hand was none too steady. When they fell together on to the bed, still fully clothed, Henry felt himself tremble. Was he about to burn a bridge that he had hitherto only set fire to in fantasyland?

'You'll muss my clothes, darling.' Janet took his head in her hands and held him till he grew more calm. 'You promised to freshen my drink, remember? Be a good boy, and get some ice while I slip into something more comfortable.'

Henry couldn't believe she had a change of clothing in her handbag.

'Like – like into what?' he asked.

'How about … like into nothing?' When she reached for the zipper on her skirt she cast him a querulous smile. 'You're not going to turn chicken on me again, are you?'

Henry hurried along the walk, peering into numerous alcoves before discovering the ice-cube dispenser alongside a battery of vending machines, all housed in a small utility room behind a glass door. Upon entering, when the door handle jiggled in his fist he wondered if it was only because his hand refused to stop shaking. He filled the bowl with ice, then concluded it was only decorous to wait a decent interval until Janet had had time to make herself ready. When he again checked his watch he realized her flight-departure time was growing closer by the minute. He grabbed the inside door handle of the utility room to make his exit. Then his eyes widened in horror. Clutched in his fist was the handle, disengaged from the door entirely.

A chill numbed him. He pushed on the door in the hope it might open out as well as in, but it only bumped defiantly against the jamb . . . . *Now don't panic, Henry. Just fit the handle back into that slot nice and easy . . . . There, that's it. Now turn it very carefully and set yourself free . . . . Oh God, now look what you've done! You've poked the handle in too far. See, you've pushed the outside handle on to the pavement . . . .* Henry buried his face in his hands. What sort of insane evening was this? Earlier he had trapped his shirt-tail in his zipper causing him to miss his flight. Now he was entombed in this stupid utility room while Janet Dunstan lay waiting – a turned-on queen in a turned-down king-size bed.

Fortunately, one possible means of escape was left open. Through the glass door he could observe a patch of lawn beyond the swimming pool where two matronly ladies stood chatting in the moonlight. If they would only glance his way he could beckon them over and report his predicament. For several minutes he waved his arms to attract their attention. But when one finally turned to face him, she drew herself up as if he were some sort of exhibitionist. Together they disappeared from sight in a huff.

Henry warned himself not to panic – surely someone would come along in need of ice or cigarettes. But another ten minutes passed before a portly gentleman approached the utility room jiggling coins in his palm. Henry leaped to the glass door like an orang-utan at the zoo.

'I'm trapped in here,' he shouted. 'Will you pick up that outside handle and open the door?'

He watched the man attempt the task, then give up with a shrug.

'Would you be good enough to go to the office,' Henry begged, 'and tell them what the problem is?'

'What *is* the problem?' asked the man.

'That I'm a prisoner and I'm innocent.' Henry couldn't imagine his situation not being obvious.

As he continued waiting he wondered whether the situation was willed to be. And would he – or could he – carry out a grand seduction here in Milwaukee while his wife's greatest sin was an occasional chocolate sundae?

Ten minutes later a sleep-infested maintenance man trudged slowly down the walk to survey the problem, then trudged away again in search of needed tools. In all, Henry spent forty minutes incarcerated before winning his freedom.

When he dashed back to his motel room he found its door standing open. Janet Dunstan was nowhere about. But the mirror revealed a boldly-scrawled message in lipstick. It read, quite simply, *Farewell chicken.*

His initial hurt ever so gradually eased itself into a feeling of relief. Yes, he could still face his wife without having proved himself unfaithful. But it was not until the morning that his purged psyche discarded its chicken image and instead took a giant macho leap forward to heights it had never before reached.

17

On his way to breakfast he could hardly wait to buy a copy of the *Milwaukee Sentinel* to see if even a short quote from his yesterday's interview had made its way into the sports section. When he reached for the top paper on the stack near the entrance to the motel's coffee-shop his hand froze in mid-air.

'Oh my God!' he cried aloud. There, big as life, he met himself face to face in the middle of the front page. Above the caption **Overjoyed Underdog** he was planting a kiss on the blade of his stubby putter, admittedly appearing a shade ridiculous but, on the other hand, displaying his new, younger image to maximum advantage.

When at last his eyes dropped to the first words of copy, he experienced yet another wave of elation at the sight of *Milwaukee (AP)*. That could mean but one thing – the Associated Press had already beamed his picture to newspapers all over the world. As he floated behind the coffee-shop hostess towards a table he could imagine Martha and her travelling companions gaping at his picture over tea in Lausanne. Even though they all would be chatting at once, Henry had no trouble in picking up his wife's broadcast frequency . . . . *Yes, Sarah, he is looking rather sporting, isn't he?* . . . . *You're so right, Mary – it's nice to know he prefers kissing putters to other women* . . . . *Oh, girls, I have this awful feeling that*

*if he's called to appear on one of those late-night talk-shows he'll
forget to ask someone to water my garden. I mean, honestly!*

After seating himself at breakfast he hurriedly unfolded his
newspaper and began reading the article; a frown crept across
his face. For one thing, the story concentrated more on the
food-poisoning incident than on Henry himself. For another,
his name had been misspelled as Summerfield. But regardless
of what had been written, wasn't it the picture itself that
would stick in people's minds? No doubt about it, his status
had been elevated overnight to that of a bona fide celebrity.

Henry felt a sudden flash of self-consciousness. What if
these dozens of patrons in the coffee-shop should start lining
up for autographs? Should he simply sign his name or instead
precede it with *Cordially* or perhaps *Best luck always*? He partly
shielded his face as he sipped his orange-juice. So this was
how it felt to be a Sinatra or a Billy Graham!

When he returned unrecognized to his motel room he felt
he had done an admirable job in concealing his identity. For
the next hour, until flight time home, he paced the floor of his
motel room trying to sort out the myriad matters demanding
his attention before he headed for the US Open in exactly one
week. He would have to write to Martha, add to his golfing
wardrobe, smooth out his swing, read up on the nature of the
Spruce Valley course, get Katie to supply him with additional
Top-Flites, make arrangements for accommodation in Denver
– the list seemed endless. But first, even before checking out
of the motel, shouldn't he buy a pair of dark glasses? it was
important that he should remain as anonymous as possible so
as not to be detained from winging his way home by a
celebrity-conscious public.

The next day, by way of proving to the world that he had not
let fame rob him of his sense of mundane responsibility, he

returned to his office at Brenham, Scofield and Meade for the purpose of determining which, if any of his clients, still desired his delayed services. But too many distractions kept him from learning the answer. His friends kept phoning their congratulations and good wishes; his fellow workers kept expressing their envy at his having the guts to wear a blazer and turtle-neck to the office. And although he couldn't swear to it, more than a few of the firm's young secretaries seemed to smile enticingly in his direction as they passed his office door on their way to coffee-break.

With more than a hint of nervousness he answered a phone message left by Jackson Johns, locally representing the United States Golf Association. Fortunately the only purpose of John's call had been to advise Henry that a single room had been reserved for him in suburban Denver beginning next Tuesday at Shadow Mountain Lodge. Just the sound of that establishment's name conjured up visions of delight in Henry's mind. He leaned back in his office chair, closed his eyes and imagined himself on the eve of the US Open leaning on the rail of the lodge's balcony with its panoramic view. With Paul Azinger at his right elbow and Tom Watson at his left, together they would watch the twilight haze settle over the Spruce Valley course far below. Both pros would silently be wishing there was some way to ease the tension of the impending Open when Henry would utter something so droll and witty that they would all chuckle, bonding themselves as permanent friends in the manner of the Three Musketeers.

On Thursday afternoon Henry had just finished composing a cablegram to Martha, advising her of his next week's Denver address, when he answered the ringing phone, assuming it would be his tailor announcing that his four new pairs of golf slacks were now altered and ready to be picked up. Instead it was a long-distance call that sent his head spinning at a dizzy pace. The caller identified himself as Bob Randall, senior editor for *Sports World* magazine, who thought Henry would be pleased to learn he was one of only five amateurs in the nation to qualify for the Open.

'Your miraculous climb in the golfing world, Mr Summerfield, has just got to be an inspiration to every one of America's thirty million ardent golfers . . . .'

Henry could not have been more flattered. 'Really? I mean, wow! . . .' He ran out of words even before getting started.

As the caller heaped one accolade on top of another Henry kept a finely-tuned ear to the receiver just to make sure it wasn't Alex Wulf disguising his voice. But the longer Henry listened, the more convinced he became that he was in fact being contacted from a switchboard in heaven itself.

'How would you like to see a *Sports World* feature story on yourself, Mr Summerfield? I'm talking about a real in-depth treatment of you at the US Open – your hopes, your frustrations, your strategy, the whole bit? Maybe three thousand words or more plus two pages of full-colour pictures. Sort of a bare-your-soul, minute-by-minute chronicle of those fabulous, traumatic days coming up for your next week at Spruce Valley . . . .'

Ten minutes later Henry hung up the phone in a trance, remembering in only the vaguest way what else it was that Bob Randall had said, and remembering not at all how he himself had replied, other than once, ever so tactfully, having clarified that his name was spelled Summer*fill*.

That evening his twelve-year-old daughter insisted on all the details.

'I suppose I should have made notes,' said Henry. 'It just came as too much of a shock, that's all.'

Katie looked at her father with her large quizzical eyes as if he were a youngster off to Cub Scout camp for the first time. 'You're sure about the procedure, Daddy? Someone from the magazine is to contact you when you arrive at the Open on Tuesday, right?'

'Right – a free-lance writer named Charles Bottomley who specializes in underdogs who have fought their way up the ladder. In fact, I guess this idea was really Bottomley's. Apparently he saw my *AP* story, and *Sports World* commissioned him to do it.' Henry searched his mind for more information to share with his daughter. 'I think Randall said that Bottomley has just flown in from Switzerland where he covered the attempt of some woman mountain-climber named Daisy to scale the north face of the Eiger. They're going to call the story *Upsie Daisy*.'

'I wonder what they will entitle the article about you?'

'I've no idea,' Henry paused and frowned. 'I just hope it won't be *The Rise and Fall of Henry the Third*.' He had no sooner uttered the words than he wondered whether he had been short-sighted in agreeing to Randall's proposition. He gazed towards Katie for counsel. 'I understand that some of these reporters are pretty merciless,' he said. 'What if Bottomley starts grilling me as to how I just happened to become, well – an overnight sensation? Sooner or later he's going to suspect that something is definitely fishy.'

'But nothing *is* fishy, Daddy. Why do I have to keep reminding you? You've simply developed a positive attitude and a smooth swing. And you use the world's only truly sensible putter.'

'But suppose he starts quizzing me about the ball?'

'Tell him you play a Top-Flite and ask if he'll talk to the Spalding people about paying you millions of dollars to endorse it.' When Henry scowled unappreciatively Katie offered him a calming smile. 'Just remember, your ball is every bit as legal as anyone else's. All you have to do in your interview sessions is to say what a wonderful bunch of guys your opponents are. Then keep repeating that you couldn't possibly have made it all the way to the Open without the unstinting help and encouragement of your wife. If nothing else, that should at least get you off the hook with Mom.'

Henry sighed deeply. How could his daughter remain so unconcerned over such a serious matter? Perhaps it was best to change the subject altogether. He asked her how she planned to spend her time at the Wulfs' while he was in Denver.

'My big goal is to see if I can hypnotize Gina. I'm studying the last of six books I borrowed from the library – *The Theory and Practice of Hypnotism* – and I think by next week I'll be ready to give it a try.'

Henry laughed aloud. 'You're something else, sweetie.' Then he grew more solemn. 'By the way, do you think you'll be OK at the Wulfs'? I mean, are you concerned about walking in your sleep?'

'Good grief, Daddy, I haven't done that for years.'

'I didn't think so but I wasn't sure.' He couldn't help but smile to recall how he had once found her at five years of age sound asleep in a chair putting together a jigsaw puzzle that had stumped Martha and him for weeks. Since that time, in typical Katie fashion, she had studied the factors involved in somnambulism so thoroughly that she could have opened her own psychiatric clinic on the subject. Now she seemed equally immersed in hypnotism. What next, he wondered? But try as he might to divert his thinking into such other-directed channels, a more immediate and foreboding thought kept chiselling away at the walls of his cerebrum.

'What's worrying you, Daddy?'

For a while he remained silent, absently stroking his new

plum-coloured pullover. 'I can't get rid of the feeling,' he said at last, 'that Charles Bottomley is going to give me a mighty hard time.'

As had been his custom for more than a month Henry struggled through the routine of his late-evening exercises, then opened Martha's bedroom wardrobe door until its full-length mirror faced towards him. Although what he was about to do caused him some inner embarrassment he reasoned that it held no aspect whatsoever of self-aggrandizement. Big-time golf, admittedly, was a no-nonsense sport. And in all fairness to its millions of television followers, wasn't it Henry's implied responsibility – just in case a camera got pointed his way – to master a few dramatic techniques, especially with regard to barely-missed putts? But was it considered ethical to imitate the routines of the more patriarchal stellar lights in the golfing constellation? Might he, for instance, be sued for plagiarism if he imitated the way Nicklaus glared at the hole as if defying it not to swallow his ball? And why Arnold Palmer had not won an Oscar, Henry would never know. Each time a Palmer putt rimmed the cup and stayed out, his initial expression of utter disbelief would dissolve into a grimace of such anguish that a first-time observer might suspect some pigmy was inside his shoes driving strips of bamboo beneath his toenails. Next Arnie would revolve his head in a slow lateral arc until he was staring at his Army behind him, his body cramped at the waist as if smitten by a karate chop to his solar plexus. It had always amazed Henry how Arnie ever survived to proceed to the next tee.

The longer Henry faced himself in the mirror the more convinced he became that in all decency he was expected to come up with an act uniquely his own. But it would need to be kept in good taste. It simply would not be within the realm of sanctioned reactions by the staid USGA for him to sink his putter blade into his caddy's skull or to hurl himself writhing and screaming on to the turf.

After an hour in front of the mirror, through trial and error he felt he had come up with an original and reasonably effective response. When the circumstances of a missed putt arose, he would, in carefully measured sequence, (a) drop his stubby putter to the green, (b) sink his head into his cupped hands, (c) shudder noticeably, (d) slowly raise his eyes and arms towards heaven, and (e) manage an eventual courageous smile as if to say, *Thy will be done*. With the aid of his stopwatch Henry timed the duration of his performance at exactly 8.4 seconds. While he might have preferred more prolonged treatments of (c) and (e), he couldn't chance having the television cameras cut away to some crass commercial about diarrhoea in the middle of his eye contact with the Lord.

Half an hour after Henry had downed a sleeping-pill and climbed into bed his eyes still refused to close, his imagination too cranked up to throw in the sponge. Now he was wishing there was some way that the playing of the national anthem could usher in each day's telecast of next week's Open. All of the players would be lined up beside the first tee in the same manner as contestants in other televised sports events stood in a row on the sidelines. The camera would pan from face to face until at last, as if striking gold, it would zoom in for a close-up of amateur Henry Summerfill. He would not be popping bubble gum nor casually shifting his weight nor mumbling half-heartedly as the band played on. No siree. He would be standing smartly to attention with his one hundred per cent linen golf cap held over his heart, enunciating each syllable so distinctly that there could be no doubt among those millions of television viewers that not only was he the sole athlete in the nation who knew all the lyrics but that he vocalized them with gusto and fervour.

When he switched off the bedside light and popped another sleeping-pill into his mouth he noticed that his hand was shaking .... *Calm down, Henry,* an inner voice counselled him. *It's too energizing for your system at bedtime to keep employing your mind as a crystal ball. Yes, I know you're enthused and excited but really, old chap, you've got to get your sleep. Stop trying to anticipate heaven. You'll be there in just a few more days ....*

Once more he flopped back on the pillows, determined to accept those words of sage advice. But the longer he lay in the night's stillness the more clearly he began to hear the ominous whisperings of that other interior voice that for so long a time had left him in peace .... *Wanna know somethin', Henry? – You couldn't be fuller of shit if you were an elephant. The only reason you keep hiding yourself in fantasies is because deep down you're so goddamn scared about competing in the Open that you've all but gone berserk. You know damn well that in spite of your miracle ball the only reason you qualified locally was because it was held on your own course. And the only reason you made it through the regional was because you gave the chicken salad a miss. Next week ain't gonna be no days of wine and roses, baby. It just may go down in history as the Great Summerfill Slaughter!*

Henry cowered under the covers and, after years of conditioned response, instinctively reached for the comfort of his wife. When he embraced nothing more than her pillow he surprised himself by calling out to her across the far Atlantic ....

'I need you, Martha, wherever you are.'

18

On Tuesday morning, in the driveway of the Summerfill residence, the taxi driver loaded Henry's $520 Italian leather golf bag and three new sizeable pieces of luggage in the boot of his cab.

'Must be quite a trip you're taking,' said the cabbie. 'Leaving for the rest of the summer?'

'Uh, not exactly.' Henry gripped the handle of his locked attaché case more firmly to ensure that he kept custody of his fresh batch of Top-Flites.

'Goodbye, Daddy. Good luck.'

'Goodbye, Katie.' For a moment he gazed into her face; her chin seemed to quiver ever so slightly. He opened his arms and felt her rush in. 'Don't let me forget I owe you for these new balls.'

'No charge this time, Daddy – not if you keep your promise to send for me on Friday if you make the cut. I want to be there to cheer you on. What's more, you need me.' Her small hand squeezed his own. 'Call me every night at the Wulfs', OK?'

'I will, Katie. I'll keep you posted on all the news.' As Henry waved farewell from inside the cab he felt bad at leaving her behind. But she had school exams to cope with so he couldn't send for her till the weekend.

More than anything he wanted to play creditably at Spruce Valley. Katie was counting on him. Martha too, perhaps. And what about his golfing buddies? How could he have guessed when Alex Wulf suggested the two of them met for a parting drink at the club that dozens of his other friends would be there too, waiting to surprise him with *For He's A Jolly Good Fellow*? Henry had never been more touched. So much so that his contact lenses had all but gone swimming away.

But today was designed for action, not nostalgia. Early this afternoon Henry would be out on the renowned Spruce Valley course tuning up for Thursday's opening round.

Henry hopscotched across the worn carpet, trying to avoid planting a foot into his opened but unpacked pieces of luggage on the motel room floor. He was searching for the diary that Bob Randall of *Sports World* had suggested he should purchase for recording titbits of information that might prove enlightening in Charles Bottomley's article. When at last Henry located it hiding beneath his new hairdryer he opened the diary at the blank first page. He pushed aside some of the paraphernalia scattered across the bed and sat down to record briefly the activities of his day since landing in Denver.

Arrived two hours late at 1:28 p.m. Left airport in rented car. Had flat tyre in centre lane of US 70 Freeway downtown. Explained to patrolman I was contestant in US Open, hoping for escort to Spruce Valley. Got ticket instead. Rode in tow truck to filling station. Arrived Spruce Valley Country Club at 3.15. Waited 25 minutes at players' registration desk while name on contestant's badge was corrected from Summerfield to Summerfill. No message from Bottomley. Told I was too late for today's practice round. Tried to get look at course but too many spectators. Only saw huge trees and knee-high rough. Asked lady at desk on which side of golf-course was Shadow Mountain Lodge. She pointed northwest. Lodge does not overlook course. Car mileage showed 9.6 miles from clubhouse. Highway under repair. Flagmen on duty. Trip took 50 minutes. Small, isolated. No restaurant facilities. Sits at base of enormous pyramid of sand and gravel used by road maintenance crews. Asked elderly desk clerk if that was Shadow Mountain. No answer; hearing aid inoperative. Heat won't turn off. TV won't turn on. Inner door to adjoining room won't close. Fortunately unoccupied. Now 8.00 p.m. Still no phone call from Bottomley. Beginning to thunder. Better find place for dinner before storm breaks . . . .

Bruno's steak house half a mile down the road featured an open charcoal grill, checked tablecloths and such minimal lighting from two wagonwheel chandeliers that even with the aid of his magnifying reading glasses Henry found it difficult to peruse the latest issue of *Golf Magazine*, which he had brought along as his dining companion.

While he waited for his dinner he gazed around the room, which was sprinkled with only a few patrons. He wondered whether by chance there could be a page missing from the programme of events handed him that afternoon at the players' registration desk. Was there some banquet he didn't know about where the other contestants were dining on pheasant? If so, was Charles Bottomley there trying to track him down?

Henry dined in silence, only vaguely mindful of the rumble of thunder as he studied *Golf Magazine*'s article previewing the US Open. And the more he read, the more convinced he grew that Spruce Valley was Hell itself simply disguised as a Garden of Eden:

> The course is more than a test of man's physical skills of strength, coordination and finesse. It is also a test of his character, his stamina, patience, daring and resolve ... Spruce Valley's full length of 6,788 yards does not strike fear into anyone's breast – not until he confronts its intimidating features – needle-narrow fairways carved out of an evergreen forest, canyon-like bunkers guarding polished-glass greens, a rushing, rugged stream whiplashing its way back and forth across a dozen holes ....

It occurred to Henry that the terrain seemed more suited to assault by battle-ready marines than by men whose only weapons were golf-clubs and a ball. When he next looked up from his magazine he all but swallowed his fork. Seated alone and facing him two tables away was a young woman so appealing in face and figure that, at the moment, Henry would not have traded places with any man on earth. As unobtrusively as possible he slipped his spectacles into his pocket, pretending to continue reading with his soft contacts alone. It mattered not that the words were a blur. What he now chose to study settled sharply into focus ten feet away.

From ingrained courtliness Henry tried not to stare, lowering his gaze with effort, her image of sensuous innocence imprinted on his mind as permanently as if his retina had snapped a Polaroid picture. Her casual flaxen hair framed an oval face aglow with the kiss of sun and wind, and her full and mobile mouth seemed alive even in repose. But what had he detected in the depths of her eyes? Frankness perhaps? Devilment? And how old was she – twenty-five ... thirty ...

116

thirty-five? Each question he posed only intensified his perplexity.

When he raised his eyes again he half suspected she had been studying him, her glance now moving past his shoulder. For one mad moment he almost confronted her with a smile but instead quickly looked away, pretending to watch the charcoal flames. He would hate making her feel uncomfortable. But brief as his second view had been, he could tell that her body was charged with a supple animal grace. Henry's breathing quickened. Not that it was a fetish with him – or was it? – but never in all his years of studied appreciation had he witnessed such perfect breasts. What's more, their exquisite buoyancy beneath her pale yellow turtle-neck – cashmere, he imagined – caused him to speculate that perhaps she was not wearing a bra. It was just one of several barely perceptible subtleties that a connoisseur on the subject – albeit a second-hand connoisseur – could not help but note, and, having noted, could never forget.

Why was she here, and what sort of note was she now writing on that pad she had pulled from her bag? An invitation for Henry to join her? He watched her intently but with discreet peripheral vision. No, she was putting the notepad away again. When their eyes met for an instant he thought he detected a wisp of a smile at the corners of her lips but he could not be sure. Again he glanced away, chiding himself for his lack of guts. He had finished his meal. Time was running out.

Did he appear to her as an upstanding not-yet-over-the-hill male whom it would be interesting to visit during dinner? Or, heaven forbid, would she interpret such an invitation as coming from a lecherous old man? Where, he wondered, did the chronological dividing line lie?

He sipped his coffee slowly, recalling the words of Alex

Wulf when the two of them had lunched together last week ...
*Hell, Henry, all this talk about people past thirty being out of it is
just a myth. Granted, you and I may look out of it to some of these
young male pups but in the eyes of the fair sex we've just hit the
prime of life. We're better lovers because we're not so quick on the
trigger, right?*

Henry felt his confidence creep up a notch. When an inner
voice began whispering he cocked his head to listen
intently .... *Why would she have chosen to sit facing you if she
didn't want your attention? She's not admiring your prim
Victorian airs. She's beginning to think the same as Janet Dunstan
– that you're a goddamn chicken. Be a man for once.*

Henry was all set to confront the situation head-on when
the young woman rose and moved to the phone booth in the
entrance alcove. He all but moaned aloud at the unpremedi-
tated provocation of her body. There, like some perfectly ordinary mortal, she began dialling a number. Could it be she'd
decided to contact another man after first having afforded
Henry the opportunity of a lifetime which he had just blown
to hell? In self-disgust he fled from Bruno's into the dark
gathering storm.

As the wind and rain launched their long-threatened assault
on Shadow Mountain Lodge, Henry sat on the side of his bed
in his pyjama bottoms staring disconsolately at the disarray of
the room. The television set was still not working and the heat
continued to pour forth as if programmed to bake a casserole.
Suddenly his psyche perked up at the prospect of now speaking to his daughter long-distance. But when he picked up the
phone he was struck down by the crowning blow of the day
– the instrument refused even to cough up a dialling tone.
Henry could not have felt more isolated if he'd been alone in
a spaceship headed for Mars.

118

For lack of anything else to do he stepped to the bathroom mirror and practised his barely-missed-putt facial expressions. In the middle of his rehearsal he was startled by a knock at the door.

He listened intently. Perhaps it had been some other sound caused by the storm. Then he heard it again, urgent and clear. Would a heating repair-man be so conscientious as to be making a call at ten o'clock at night?

He unbolted the latch and slowly edged the door open with only his head peeking around it so as not to reveal that he was clad only in his pyjama bottoms. When he stared at the person on the rain-swept porch he clutched the doorknob more tightly for support. There with her breasts sculpted against her drenched pale yellow turtle-neck stood the young woman from the steak-house.

'Mr Summerfill?'

'Yes,' he managed at last.

'Hi. I'm Charlie Bottomley . . . . Well ... may I come in?'

19

Henry scrambled into his bathrobe, then handed a towel to his female night visitor. Even though she had slipped and fallen while racing to his room she smiled in good humour as she dried her face and hair. Now her enormous blue eyes peeked out at him from behind the towel.

'You looked so shocked to find me at the door,' she said. 'Surely Bob Randall didn't imply you should expect a man!'

Henry tried to hark back to his last week's conversation with the senior editor of *Sports World*.

'Now that you mention it, I don't recall that he referred to you as either he or she. I just, well, naturally assumed that – that—'

'—that I was a male, right?' She pursed her lips in exasperation. 'You can't imagine how awkward it is to be named Charles. How would *you* like to be named Mary?'

'I see your point,' he said.

'Before I was born as a fifth daughter, my father was so anxious for a boy that he referred to me as Charlie. And he was too stubborn to change my name after I popped into the world. I apologize for being so late, Mr Summerfill, but I've been trying since noon to track you down. Is your phone out of order?'

'I'm afraid so.' He wished his pulse wouldn't race so out of control.

'Wasn't that a coincidence about our seeing each other at Bruno's? Or didn't you even notice me there?'

'Oh, yes,' Henry admitted. 'I definitely noticed.'

'You didn't appear to. Most men want to buy me a drink.'

'I didn't want to seem too forward.'

She laughed aloud. 'I doubt that you've ever been guilty of that.'

Was she too implying he was a chicken? He tried not to notice that her cashmere sweater had already begun shrinking as she launched into an explanation of why she had been unable to contact him earlier. After arriving late at the airport she had hired a car and sped to a motel six blocks from the golf course where Bob Randall had assured her he had reserved a room in her name. But when she had tried to check in, not only did they not have her reservation but they didn't know of any other motel with a possible vacancy. In spite of scouring every lodging establishment within a ten-mile radius of Spruce Valley, she still remained without accommodation. Meantime, after having learned from the players' registration desk that Henry was staying at Shadow Mountain Lodge she had raced in and out of phone booths trying to reach him. But always there had been an engaged tone. She had finally driven here an hour ago and knocked on his door. When there was no answer she decided to find a place for dinner and try later. While at Bruno's she had again tried to phone but with the same frustrating result. After finishing her meal she decided to knock on his motel room door one more time, stepping from her car just as the storm unleashed its fury.

'So here I am,' she said, 'a cold wet puppy with no place to stay.'

Despite the uncontrollable heat of the room, Henry felt himself shiver as he pointed towards the sprung inner door. 'The room that adjoins mine is vacant,' he heard himself. 'You could spend the night there. The door between the rooms won't altogether close but – well, you can trust me, Miss Bottomley. Or is it Mrs?'

'It's Ms,' she answered. 'Big M, little s. But I'd rather you called me Charlie.'

'And I'd rather you called me Henry,' he ventured.

On inspection it became immediately apparent why the next-door room was vacant. While it contained a made-up bed together with a mish-mash of other furniture crowded against one wall, most of the floor area was taken over by paint cans and other sundry maintenance equipment. Its bathroom, seemingly destined for oblivion, had been stripped of all fixtures.

'At least there's a bed,' she said. 'That's all I need – I hope you won't mind my sharing your bath. In fact, it it's not too much of an imposition, right now a hot shower is just what I need.'

When she reached for the bottom of her sweater as if to peel it off Henry's eyes all but leaped from their sockets. So as not to seem a voyeur he quickly moved to the window and peered out into the rain.

'Before you start your shower, why don't you tell me where you parked your car. I'll get your bags so you'll have some-thing dry to change into.'

'I guess I forgot to tell you about my luggage. It just plain hasn't arrived yet. For all I know it may be on a jet headed for China.' Her voice grew softly pleading. 'You didn't bring along a second bathrobe, did you?'

'Golly, Charlie, if I'd only known!'

'An extra pair of pyjamas maybe?'

'I, uh, only brought bottoms. But don't worry about it,' he said. 'I'll find you something.' After she had closed the bathroom door and begun her shower, he rummaged among his voluminous wardrobe for items best suited for temporary feminine attire. The nearest thing to a bathrobe, he decided, was his raincoat. And, yes, she could wear a pair of his pyjama bottoms if she used one of his neckties as a belt. But what could he substitute for a pyjama top? He found the perfect item half hidden under his USGA rule book – the translucent forty-five dollar long-sleeved silk undershirt he had ordered for winter golf.

Henry picked up his armful of selected apparel. 'I have some things for you to wear,' he called through the bathroom door.

When she cracked it open and extended a naked, lissom arm, Henry draped the clothes across her wrist.

'What's the raincoat for?' she asked. 'Is the roof leaking?'

'That's all I could find as a substitute robe.'

'How about the necktie? Are we expecting company?'

When he advised her of its intended purpose as a belt, she complimented him on his inventiveness. Behind the bathroom door she began humming again, then paused.

'Get set for our first interview, Henry. I can't wait to discover the secret of how you got so good at golf so fast.'

He was still cautioning himself not to panic when she appeared before him. She pirouetted across the room modelling her makeshift ensemble, appearing for all the world like a freshly-scrubbed little girl playing at dressing-up in her daddy's borrowed clothes. But her smile was so direct and her eyes so filled with the aura of womanhood that his hormones at once began to stir. She pulled a notebook and pen from her shoulder bag on the dressing-table.

'All right,' she said, suddenly businesslike, 'why don't you start by telling me what thoughts ran through your mind when you first decided to try to qualify for the Open.'

'Well, it really wasn't my own idea,' he began. 'I have this friend, Alex Wulf, who . . . .'

'Excuse me,' she interrupted, 'but is it as warm in here as I think? I'm practically roasting.'

'The heat won't turn off,' he said.

'You mean there's no way to cool off the room? Can't you switch to air-conditioning?'

'I've tried that. The heat just pours out faster.'

She got up and opened the outside door. When the wind and rain swept into the room, she quickly closed it. For a while she stood before him studying his face.

'Henry,' she said at last, 'I'm about to do something purely for the sake of comfort. So don't panic, OK?' Even before she finished speaking she began unbuttoning the raincoat. In another moment she faced him clad only in his baggy pyjama bottoms and the silk T-shirt, the latter hiding almost nothing at all.

The ensuing interview on Henry's ascendancy in the golfing world lasted for more than an hour. But he scarcely remained aware of what she had asked or how he had answered. Although it had yet to show up on a physical exam he felt convinced his wiring system had somehow become short-circuited during adolescence with the result that the finer messages of his mind kept getting jammed by static interference from his gonads. Only vaguely did he recall confessing to having once signed up for a correspondence course in muscle maintenance and having been promptly laid up with a pulled tendon. The following winter he had tried strengthening his legs by pulling firewood around the garden on a sled. Instead he had come down with pneumonia. Henry noticed that the faster he talked the more hastily Charlie scribbled in her notebook. And the more hastily she scribbled, the more emphatically her breasts jiggled.

'I think we'd better call it a night,' she said finally. 'My fingers are worn to the bone.' She shut her notebook and smiled up at him. 'How are you enjoying it so far, Henry?'

'Funny,' he said, 'I'm not a bit tired.'

Before she retired past the open door to her bed, she paused to rummage through her handbag on the dressing-table, at last extracting a small bottle that contained a solitary pill. She downed it with a glass of water.

'Remind me to try to get my prescription refilled tomorrow,' she said. 'It's important.'

Soon after, as he lay awake staring at the ceiling, Henry wondered if her remark about her prescription was in reference to birth-control pills. If so, what was she trying to tell him? He flopped nervously on his bed. Was it actually true that young women preferred older men? And was he the only US Open contestant who was not tonight treating himself to the therapeutic benefits of pre-tournament sex? In the overwhelming awareness of Charlie's nearby presence, Henry at last fell asleep, all but forgetting that tomorrow was his only day to practise on the treacherous Spruce Valley course before the beginning of the Open itself.

20

Henry was midway through his morning shower when he was startled by a knock at the bathroom door.

'Telephone,' he heard Charlie shout above the roar of water. 'It's your wife calling from Italy.'

Henry leaped from the shower and hastily half dried himself. When did the phone start working, he wondered, and what sort of emergency had prompted Martha to call? He pulled on his robe and raced to the bedside phone . . . .

'Hello.'

'Henry, is that you?'

'Yes, dear . . . . is everything all right?'

Apparently she preferred him to answer a question of hers first.

'Henry, who in the world answered the phone?'

Henry hesitated uncomfortably. 'That was – uh – Charles Bottomley, the sports writer. Or haven't you had my letter about my being interviewed by *Sports World* magazine?'

'Yes, Henry, I did get the letter but . . . .'

'Where in Italy are you, Martha?'

She did not say Rome or Florence or Venice. She said: 'Is Charles Bottomley as effeminate as he sounds?'

'Yes. I mean, no. I mean, yes.' Henry couldn't help but

notice the smile of amusement on Charlie's face as she turned back towards her room. Henry groped for words that would direct his phone conversation into safer channels . . . . 'Have you visited a spaghetti factory yet, sweetheart? Are Italian men really fanny pinchers, ha-ha?'

'Henry, what's wrong with you?'

'Nothing's wrong. I'm just curious about your trip.'

'Henry, why did it take you so long to answer the phone?'

'I was taking a shower.'

'And was Charles Bottomley interviewing you in the shower? I mean, *honestly.*'

'It's very complicated, Martha. I don't think we can afford to discuss it at overseas telephone rate . . . . Is your money holding out all right, dear?'

'Yes, I think so.'

From where Henry sat he chanced to see Charlie's reflection in a mirror through the open door between the two rooms. When suddenly she slipped out of her raincoat, nude from the waist up, he all but passed out cold . . . .

His wife's voice seemed not a part of the real world at all.

'Henry, are you there? ... hello ... hello . . . .'

'Uh – yes. Yes, Martha, I'm here ...'

'We must have a bad connection, Henry. You almost sound like you're gasping. By the way, what time is it in Denver? I get confused about time zones.'

'It's exactly seven-fifteen.'

'In the morning or evening?'

'In the morning, dear.'

'Isn't that rather early for an interview? Or is Mr Bottomley sharing your room?'

'Look, Martha, let's talk about *you*, OK? Was Portofino the charming little fishing village you hoped it would be?' When, quite by accident, Henry caught another mirrored glimpse of

127

Charlie's flawless breasts he felt his head spin uncontrollably . . . . 'How are your boobies, Martha?' No sooner had that inane Freudian slip passed his lips than he fought desperately to cover his mistake. 'Movies, Martha – have you seen any movies?' The silence seemed endless.

'Henry,' his wife said at last, 'could you possibly have suffered a stroke?'

'Look, dear, I'm in great shape. Except that I'm under all sorts of pressure here at the Open.' He tried to adopt a more jocular attitude. 'Come on,' he coaxed, 'give me a rundown on what's cooking in Europe.'

She seemed not even to hear him. 'Tell me more about Charles Bottomley.'

While Henry remained not guilty of any indiscretion, he saw no point in clouding the issue by revealing that Charlie was female. He could better explain that at a later time. On the other hand, Henry felt it wisest not to trap himself by perpetrating blatant lies. Perhaps, as Bob Randall of *Sports World* had so artfully managed to do, Henry could simply refrain from any he or she references in answering his wife's persistent enquiries.

'Charlie is staying in the room next to mine,' he explained, 'and there's an inner door between the rooms. Charlie heard the phone while I was in the shower and answered it.'

'Is he standing within earshot now?'

'No, Charlie has returned to – uh – Charlie's own room.'

'Poor Henry, the tournament does have you all flustered, doesn't it?'

'I'd better go now,' he said. 'I've got to hurry to Spruce Valley and get in some last-minute practice. Oh, incidentally, Martha, I've got some terrific news for you – your flowers are being watered every day . . . . Goodbye, dear.'

At nine that morning Henry pulled his car to a stop in the parking lot of the Spruce Valley Country Club. Charlie had decided to remain behind at Shadow Mountain Lodge working on her story and trying to track down her lost luggage by telephone.

With his contestant's badge pinned to his sweater Henry acknowledged the salute given to him as he moved through a gate into an area restricted solely to players and caddies. With a surprising bounce to his walk he stepped inside the starters' tent to enquire as to the tee-off time that had been assigned to him for his practice round on the final day before the tournament began tomorrow. Nor could he resist asking the identity of his playing mates, half fearful yet half hoping that by chance, when the names of the tournament players were drawn from a hat for practice-round pairings, he might find himself playing with a couple of the top stars.

The starter ran his finger down two long columns of names, then scratched his head.

'What time did you request?' he asked.

'I didn't,' Henry said. 'Yesterday a lady at the registration desk told me that today's practice round would be prearranged for everyone, and that I should check with you as to when I was to play, and with whom.'

The starter promptly advised Henry that the lady at the registration desk, whoever she was, obviously didn't know her ass from her elbow, and that each contestant was responsible for organizing his own game. The starter further advised Henry that unfortunately there were no tee-off times left nor even any other contestants who were without a game.

Henry turned away, confused and dejected, and made his way back inside the clubhouse to the grill-room.

After finishing a cup of coffee he stared for some time into the bottom of his cup, then decided that he could make the most productive use of his time by hitting balls on the practice range situated on the far side of the press tent. He retrieved half a dozen of his clubs and set forth in that direction. He was passing the entrance of the press tent when two men emerged in matching blue blazers followed by a covey of reporters. The two men, Henry surmised, were officials of the USGA, and they were adamantly defending the degree to which they had toughened up the Spruce Valley course for the Open tournament.

'We're not trying to victimize the world's best golfers,' one of the officials said, sucking on his pipe. 'We're simply trying to find out who the best golfers really are. It's true, this is no course for the unskilled shotmaker. If there are any of that sort of players around, they're in for some mighty anguishing hours.'

Henry quickened his step, anxious to remove himself from earshot of such frightening pronouncements. But before he could escape completely, he overheard the other official state that the greens would be cut down to nine sixty-fourths of an inch. That, mused Henry to himself, was about as close as a man could shave with a Gillette Sensor razor.

When he rounded the corner of the press tent and viewed the practice range, he stopped dead in his tracks. How could he have been so foolish as to have assumed it would be deserted? Not only was it crowded with fellow contestants but it was ringed by spectators who were oo-ing and ah-ing at the shots that boomed forth all but out of sight from the practice-tee into the blue Colorado sky.

After an attendant handed him a bucket of red-striped range balls, Henry waited for a teeing area to be vacated. And the longer he waited, all the while marvelling at the shots of the other contestants, the more uncomfortable he began to feel about publicly exhibiting his own swing. Without his specially treated Top-Flites, his best drive would travel no farther than the eight-irons that Tiger Woods was hitting near where Henry waited. Suddenly he pretended his name was being called on an intercom from the press tent. He quickly picked up his clubs, nodded briefly to the crowd, then disappeared.

21

Henry called his daughter late that afternoon on the eve of the first round from a phone booth in the Spruce Valley Clubhouse.

'Yes, Katie,' he said after they had talked for a few minutes, 'I couldn't agree with you more. It does seem unfair that I'll have to start competing tomorrow without once having played the course. If that lady at the registration desk yesterday hadn't seemed so positive that . . . .'

'But Daddy, haven't you learned to expect ineptness in people? Why didn't you double check what she told you? Oh, I just knew I should have flown out there with you. Didn't you get in any practice at all?'

His daughter sounded so distressed that he tried making light of his predicament.

'Sure I practised, sweetie. It wasn't a lost day by any means. I hit practice balls all afternoon.' Henry stopped short of advising his twelve-year-old that all of his practice had been conducted at a public roadside golf range on the far side of Denver where the only other patron was an anaemic-looking young man with a pierced eyebrow and a tattoo of roses. Henry had found his presence disconcerting in the extreme – not so much because of the fellow's non-golfing appearance

132

but because he kept hitting shots consistently longer than Henry's, even while munching on a Big Mac.

'Are you feeling all right, Daddy?' his daughter was saying.

'Fine.'

'And you say your chats with Charles Bottomley are going along OK – that's great. Is he a nice guy?'

'Uh, Charles is real nice, yes . . . . Oh, say, Katie, I've got to run now. They're beginning to post the first round tee-off times. Wish me luck, sweetie. I'll call you tomorrow as soon as it's over . . . .'

Although it had taken Charlie most of the day, she had at last tracked down and claimed her missing baggage, but she had still been unsuccessful in finding another motel room.

'I guess you'll just have to put up with me a little longer,' she said when Henry returned late that afternoon. While the fact that she would be spending another night or two amid a floorful of paint cans didn't seem to bother her, she expressed dismay, if only briefly, that she must have lost the prescription she needed to replenish her now-exhausted supply of pills.

'Oh, well,' she said, shrugging, 'I shouldn't need one tonight anyway.' She hesitated, then addressed him more directly. 'Sometimes I walk in my sleep. The pills keep me from doing that. The only reason I'm even mentioning it is because of the way our rooms open on to each other. If by some chance you should hear me walking around, just ignore it. I never fail to return to my bed.'

'Maybe I can help you, Charlie. I have some super-strong sleeping pills that I'll take in case I can't sleep because of the excitement of the tournament.'

'Thanks anyway but I don't think that would help. My pills aren't really for making me sleep. Instead they're for tran-quillizing my pontine reticular responses, whatever those are.' She smiled at his frown of concern. 'Don't worry Henry. I'll probably sleep snug as a kitten.'

Now, several hours later, following another lengthy evening interview, Henry tossed restlessly in bed, flopping and turning in the pale moonlight that seeped through the venetian blinds of his room. More than two hours had passed since they had said goodnight and turned out the lights in their respective rooms. Even if Henry were able to doze off at once, he would not get even six hours of sleep. That was because he had been forced to set his alarm for 5.45. Why so early? Because unfortunately he was scheduled to tee off in the US Open at the ungodly hour of 7.20 in the morning.

For the past several minutes he had debated whether to down one of those as yet untried potent sleeping pills. But he was hesitant to do so in view of his having to start play in so short a time, when he would need to be more alert than ever before in his life.

Henry gazed at the open door frame to the adjoining darkened room. Although last night's heating situation had been remedied, the same could not be said of the warped door. For the sake of Charlie's privacy he had requested that it should be made to close and lock. But the carpenter who had arrived while both Henry and Charlie were gone during the day had removed the door altogether, transporting it away from the premises to perform his corrective surgery. Now the door apparently still remained in intensive care somewhere within the man's woodworking shop. It made Henry wonder if his inability to sleep was generated as much by Charlie's open-door nearness as by the moment of golfing truth that was fast reaching out to claim him.

The more vigorously Henry ordered himself to sleep, the more tense he grew. He shut his eyes so tight that little green stars began swimming on the backs of his eyelids. He flopped from his back on to his stomach, then repeated the routine three more times in quick succession. With a sudden moan of defeat he climbed from bed, made his way to the bathroom and removed a small bottle from his toilet case. *Let's see,* he reasoned, *if I took two of these sleeping pills instead of one, wouldn't that cause me to go to sleep twice as fast and sleep twice as soundly? And if I slept twice as soundly, wouldn't that convert my possible remaining four and a half hours of sleep into the equivalent of nine hours? And if I slept nine hours, wouldn't I wake up rested and refreshed?* When the more rational side of his mind was too pooped to offer its rebuttal he popped a pair of the quick-acting sleeping-pills into his mouth.

Climbing back under the sheet once again, Henry propped the pillow under his head and lay on his back waiting for the pills to work their magic. Sure enough, he soon felt his eyelids grow so heavy so fast it almost frightened him. Before they closed completely, he glanced towards his bedside clock for one final fuzzy check of the time. With an effort he noted that it was exactly 1.30. Then he noted something even more alarming – Charlie Bottomley was gliding through the doorway in a nightie that hardly existed at all.

She moved slowly in the moonlit haze of the room, gracefully, almost as if in a trance. She stood still as a statue for nearly a minute, then turned towards his bed. In the milky-soft surrealistic light he observed the full rounded form of her breasts. Ah, such beautiful living things, trembling in the flash of perfection!

Now she was but a step away. A tender moon-shadow rested on her cheek. The long thin curve of her eyelids accentuated the delicacy of her face . . . . Henry felt wave after wave of goose-pimples creep up his spine. He asked himself if he was already asleep and dreaming, and yet somehow he knew this was for real.

She was looking down at him with quiet, open eyes. His heart stopped for a long moment, then raced to catch up. She shook back a strand of golden hair and seated herself on his bed. Her nostrils flared as if in the heat of a passionate dream.

His toes curled under until they ached. His mouth turned dry as cottonwool, and his head began spinning out of control. He tried to reach out to her but already his arms had grown too heavy .... *Good God, Henry,* his inner voice screamed at him, *why in hell did you take those sleeping pills?*

Only in an other-world sort of way was he mindful that her fingers were walking down across his body as if it were the Yellow Pages. He struggled to stay awake but already the battle was lost – he went tumbling, tumbling, tumbling down into a lost world of sleep.

22

In the pale light of morning Henry pulled his windbreaker more closely around him, inhaling deeply of the chill mountain air to help sweep the cobwebs from his sleep-befogged mind. In another ten minutes, at exactly 7.20, he would be called to the tee to fire the initial salvo of the United States Open. While Henry realized that being the first contestant to tee off was in no way equivalent to earning the pole position at the Indianapolis 500, he could at least claim the distinction – assuming he survived to tell it – at having got this momentous sporting event under way. He attempted to ignore a sadistic thought that he had pecked at a corner of his brain since midway through his morning orange juice: What if he should miss his tee shot altogether! When a terrible weakness attacked his knees, he closed his eyes and tried to redirect his thinking away from such a possible impending disaster. But his internal channel selector garbled that bit of trauma with a rerun of another sort – that of Charlie Bottomley's finger dance on his belly just as his master fuse had snuffed out all the lights in his consciousness. A few hours later, when his alarm had sounded, she had shaken him awake and aimed him towards an ice-cold shower. By then she was modestly clad in a woolly robe and telling him that she had slept like a log from the moment her head had hit the pillow.

Henry appraised the scene around him. With the Spruce Valley Clubhouse shrouded in fog like a haunted mansion, the setting seemed more appropriate for a gothic novel than the United States Open. Yesterday the clubhouse and grounds had swarmed with spectators, contestants, members of the press and USGA officials. That's the way it would be again soon. But now, at ten past seven, the only other characters who shared the premises with Henry – all transfixed in a ghost-like aura – were a few caddies, half a dozen USGA officials and a smattering of early-starting golfers, none of whom he recognized either by sight or name.

Henry shifted his gaze past a recently erected television tower towards the course itself where the fairways lay hushed beneath the silver dew. Wisps of fog, like giant cobwebs, clung to the terrible towering trees that stood defiantly in every direction. In the morning stillness he could hear the rushing of Cherokee Creek that posed its own menacing hazard on nearly half the holes on the course. All too soon he, Henry Summerfill the Third, a very ordinary mortal with a high handicap and a small supply of doctored golf balls, would be competing in a tournament against the world's greatest golfers. But, like Henry, the other two members of his own threesome had yet to reach that sort of recognition. They were both young club pros – Buzzy Bressler, from Okmulgee, Oklahoma, and J.D. Holly from Prairie Village, Kansas.

With mounting nervousness Henry was gazing down the narrow tree-lined first fairway – a 390-yard par-four hole – when a voice blared over the loudspeaker:

THE FIRST ROUND OF THIS UNITED STATES OPEN

WILL NOW GET UNDER WAY. ON THE TEE PLEASE –
HENRY SUMMERFILL, AMATEUR....

Henry felt his feet propel him up on to the elevated tee. Was
it possible that the beat of his heart could be heard all the way
to downtown Denver? A jumble of ludicrous thoughts leaped
to his mind. Should he, in response to the starter's announcement, clasp his hands over his head in the manner of a prize-
fighter? Should he bow from the waist like Van Cliburn about
to give a concert? More to the point, what were his chances of
shanking his tee shot, knocking the pipe from the mouth of
that chubby USGA official off to the right? As Henry leaned
over to tee up his ball he dredged up a line from a stanza that
had slept unnudged in his memory since high school: *There is
no way out, there is no way back, there is no other way but
through* . . . .

Never had Henry's relief been greater than when his drive
split the centre of the fairway, respectably in play. And yet, as
he stepped back waiting for Bressler and Holly to hit, he
couldn't help but notice that the smattering of people around
the tee seemed to be staring at him oddly as if wondering how
any golfer with that sort of weak, disjointed, middle-aged
swing could have earned a competing berth here at the
world's greatest tournament.

Both Bressler and Holly slammed their drives off the tee
with such force that the crack of the club-head against the ball
reverberated like a rifle-shot in the nearby pines. While their
shots sailed far past Henry's, both of their balls suffered the
misfortune of being hit so far that they ended up in the fairway bunker some 260 yards from the tee.

Henry's second shot, a three-wood, alighted short of the
green but bounced nicely on to the putting surface, stopping
twenty-five feet from the hole from which point he two-
putted for his par-four. But neither Bressler nor Holly

managed to hit the green from their lies close under the lip of the fairway trap. And when they each garnered a bogey-five, Henry's psyche revved itself up a notch. At the moment, he was leading the United States Open.

After playing half a dozen holes a few surprisingly happy facts began to dawn on Henry concerning the treacherous Spruce Valley course. While it was laid out in such a manner as to prove exceedingly difficult to any golfer who could pump out his drive 240 yards or more, it offered little in the way of obstacles to Henry's shorter range off the tee. Most fairways, for example, had been narrowed considerably to between 225 and 290 yards out from the tee. Any golfer driving his ball that distance but failing to keep it straight would find his shot either in a deep fairway trap or in six inches of wiry rough. But since even Henry's best drive would come to rest well short of those troublesome areas he did not fall heir to the difficult recovery shots that both Bressler and Holly were forever being forced to attempt, too often without success.

The par-five seventh hole, with Cherokee Creek rushing across the fairway just short of the green itself, flung down an intriguing gauntlet to almost every other Open contestant. One could reach the green with two superb shots, gunning for a birdie or even possibly an eagle. The less bold could play the hole more conservatively with a drive and an iron into a landing area short of the creek. From that point a soft wedge could be lofted to the green for an almost sure par or a possible likely birdie. Neither Bressler nor Holly, like the majority of players to follow, could resist the temptation to go for the green on their second shots. But due to the distortion of the mountains as a backdrop, the far bank of the creek appeared closer than it really was. Consequently, both ended up in Cherokee Creek. Henry, on the other hand, was able to hit a

140

full fairway wood for his second shot, knowing he would still find himself several yards short of the hazard. From there he stroked a six-iron into the green and made a routine par while each of his playing mates were lucky to salvage bogeys.

When his threesome finished the first nine Henry found himself only two over par at thirty-seven while neither Bressler nor Holly had broken forty. It was a circumstance that made Henry feel almost apologetic about not being able to hit the ball far enough to get into the sort of trouble the USGA had so sadistically engineered.

He was sipping a Coke, making ready to start out on the back side when he felt a tap on his shoulder. It was Charlie Bottomley in a snug sweater-and-pants outfit announcing she was going to tag along as his personal gallery for the concluding nine holes of the day. The stimulation caused by the visible rhythm of her moving parts so unnerved each member of the threesome that, on the tenth tee, Bressler hooked his drive out of bounds, Holly pushed his tee shot into Cherokee Creek and Henry topped his own shot so badly that it dribbled less than a hundred yards ahead. As she walked beside him, the resilience of the turf seemed to put an added spring into her step. The result was a transfer of energy upwards to her marvellous breasts, which began quivering in such a manner that Henry felt himself fast losing his powers of golfing concentration. Because of it he joined Bressler and Holly in bogeying the tenth, eleventh and twelfth holes.

'I think I'm bad luck for you,' Charlie whispered to him as they walked towards the thirteenth tee. 'I'd better head back to the clubhouse and wait for you there.'

From that point on Henry managed to regain his concentration. He plugged along in unspectacular fashion, hitting his share of sub-standard shots but at the same time, because of his extraordinary putting with his miracle ball, he was able to put together a steady string of pars. On the eighteenth green, just after he had crouched over his stubby putter and sunk his putt, a steady gale-force wind swept in across the course to start giving fits to those 147 other golfers behind him. Had Henry personally been in charge of the great Rocky Mountain wind machine, he could not have picked a more strategic moment to turn it up to full speed.

Late that afternoon Henry phoned his daughter long-distance from the Spruce Valley Clubhouse. He informed her as calmly as he was able that he had not altogether disgraced himself. Relative to the rest of the field his seventy-four was a fairly decent score. It was in fact lower than the average first-round score of seventy-five. On the other hand, there were thirty-seven other scores as low or lower than Henry's. The only bit of information he neglected to mention to Katie was that the wind played havoc with every threesome other than his own.

'Just hang in there tomorrow,' she cried with enthusiasm, 'and you'll make the cut for sure. If you do, you're going to send for me, remember? I'm all packed and ready.'

After cautioning his daughter against such false optimism he ever so slightly edged the conversation into an avenue of mounting concern for him now that night-time was fast approaching.

'Are you sleeping all right, Katie? I mean, you haven't walked in your sleep there at the Wulfs', have you?'

'Oh, Daddy, you know I haven't done that for years.' There was a pause on the line. 'Incidentally, are *you* sleeping all right?'

'Well, I ... I ....'

'Something's wrong, isn't it?'

'No, not really, Katie. I mean, not exactly .... It's just that, well, Charlie Bottomley is a sleep-walker.'

142

'Really? But what's that got to do with you?'

Henry realized he could not expect to gain information without first imparting some. 'Charlie occupies the room adjoining mine at Shadow Mountain Lodge.'

'So?'

'Well, Katie, this may sound screwy but there's no door between our rooms. When Charlie sleep-walks it ... has a tendency to keep me awake.'

'You mean he sleep-walks from his room into yours?'

'That's right.'

'Have you caught him going through your wallet?'

'Oh, no, nothing like that.'

'You're leading up to something, Daddy. What is it?'

Henry took a deep breath before answering. 'Perhaps I shouldn't tell you this, Katie ... but, well ... Charlie Bottomley is a she.'

'Oh, wow!'

'Believe me, Katie, I had no idea of it until she knocked on my door the night before last. It was then she told me she had nowhere to stay. There was this vacant room next to mine and—'

'I have the feeling she's young and attractive. Right, Daddy?'

'Uh, yes. Yes, quite.'

'Hmmmm. And she walked in her sleep into your room?'

'I'm afraid that's right, yes. But today she doesn't remember that she did.'

In the phone booth Henry shifted from one foot to the other, feeling it inappropriate to reveal any more details to his twelve-year-old daughter. Even so, he was anxious to gain some insight as to the motivation for his suite-mate's mysterious night-time visit. 'I know you've made a complete study of sleep-walking, Katie. Maybe you could clue me in on ....'

He didn't know how best to continue.

'First of all, Daddy, can you tell if she's exhibiting evidence of telencephalic sleep or rhonbencephalic sleep? It's possible, of course, that it could simply be one of the milder forms of *pavor nocturnes*, which is more—'

'Katie,' he broke in, 'let's not play word games, OK?'

'But I'm only trying to define the issue. If you'd be more specific, maybe I could help with what's bothering you.'

'All right,' Henry said, clearing his throat. 'Is it possible, as a general rule—'

'General rules are beside the point, Daddy. Psychogenic behaviour concerns departures from the general rule. Now what exactly is your question?'

Henry hesitated for some time. 'Is it possible,' he said at last, 'for a sleep-walker to carry out certain ... uh, physical actions ... while asleep and not remember them later?'

'What are you trying to tell me?' Katie's curiosity seemed piqued.

'Nothing in particular.'

'Oh, yes you are ... she made sexual advances, am I correct?'

Henry could hardly believe this sort of conversation was generating between him and his twelve-year-old child.

'Katie, I'm completely innocent. I swear.'

'I never once doubted that, Daddy.'

'Even so, it's not the sort of thing I want your mother to learn about. I mean—'

'Oh, I understand that ... oh, yes indeedie I do.'

'I mean, it's just that ... well, wives tend to sometimes misconstrue—'

'As to Charlie's actions,' broke in Katie, 'you're probably wondering if she really sleep-walked last night or just faked it. Actually, it could be either.' Katie hesitated. 'Please don't be shocked with my questions, Daddy, but while you believed her to be in that somnambulant state, did the two of you perform a, you know … sexually climactic act?'

'Katie!'

'Well, did you?'

When he spoke his voice was hardly a whisper. 'I don't think so.'

'You don't *think* so?'

Henry winced painfully. 'I – well, I fell asleep.'

'You're kidding! I mean, I've never experienced that sort of thing myself but from what I've read on the subject, I thought . . . .'

'Where would you have read things of that nature?' he demanded, hopeful of transferring the monkey from his back to hers.

'I'll tell you where I read it,' she struck back. 'I read it in a big fat explicitly illustrated book entitled *The Joy of Sex.*'

'And just where, young lady, would you run across that sort of smutty material?'

'In Mom's bottom desk-drawer, that's where. Last week I was looking for some stationery and—'

'*That* book? In your *mother's* possession?' Henry felt breathless. 'Someone must have smuggled it there. Like maybe the cleaning woman. Really, Katie, when it comes to, uh, that sort of thing, I doubt that your mother is even aware of—'

'Oh, you men are so smug! Maybe Mom is more enlightened than you suspect.'

For just an instant Henry had an insane vision of Martha engaged in group sex in a Venetian gondola. He shook his head to clear it.

'Let's get back to Charlie Bottomley,' he said into the phone. 'Now that we seem to be discussing things quite openly, would you say that it is or is not possible for a sleep walker to engage in — or perhaps I should say, *initiate* – as you put it, a sexually climactic act?'

'I can only tell you what I've read, Daddy. The biological wish to sleep can be impeded by even stronger desires attached to unfulfilled emotional needs. Thus, certain sexual actions that a person might reject on a conscious level – perhaps because of rigid moral training – might be released in a somnambulistic state. Even so, that person will never do anything counter to his or her natural subconscious inclinations.'

Henry pressed the receiver closer to his ear, waiting for his encyclopaedic daughter to home in on one tangible, irrefutable, yes-or-no answer so that he might then form a studied opinion as to whether Charlie had or had not raped him last night.

'Rhonbencephalic sleep,' his daughter was saying, 'also called the paradoxical phase, consists of cortical arousal, extreme muscular relaxation and raised thresholds.'

'Katie.'

'Jouvet has studied that phenomenon in cats and finds that it is also accompanied by twitches of the vibrissae and by cardio-vascular variations.'

'Katie, please . . . .'

'Of course Jouvet isn't the only authority, Daddy. Maslow and Mittelminn hold slightly different points of view, while Rechtschaffen believes that . . . .'

'Katie,' he interjected forcefully, 'I see Charlie coming across the clubroom now and you still haven't told me whether anything like that could have happened last night.'

'Maybe yes, maybe no. You see, Daddy, the pathology of sleep is a scientific frontier laced with so many dark and winding tunnels that . . . .'

When Charlie poked her smiling face into the phone booth,

146

Henry hung up with a quick goodbye. If he was destined to learn the truth about Charlie's unusual nocturnal habits, he supposed he would have to play the role of a shrewd detective all by himself.

23

'Goodnight, Henry.'

'Goodnight, Charlie.'

Henry felt his pulse quicken – the moment he had been anticipating had at last arrived. During and since dinner Charlie had interviewed him at length. Now she laid aside her notebook and stretched in the open doorway between their rooms. Tomorrow she would be moving on. The Holiday Inn had found a place for her.

'I'm sorry those paint buckets haven't been removed from your floor,' he said to her.

'No big deal.' She shook out her straw-coloured hair and smiled. 'I've appreciated your letting me stay here, Henry. I'm afraid I'd feel terribly nervous in a similar situation with almost any other man. You just can't imagine what beasts they can be. With you it's different.'

Henry wasn't sure whether to take her remark as a compliment or a put-down.

'Are you calling me a chicken, Charlie?'

'Oh, Henry, heavens no. I think you're quite macho.'

He suspected she might be teasing.

'Last night,' he said defensively, 'I was knocked out by those sleeping pills.'

She cocked her head quizzically. 'What do you mean by that?'

Henry looked into her face, but when her expression gave no hint of comprehension, he dropped his eyes. Perhaps in truth she had no recollection of having come to his bedside at all. But in case she was only feigning innocence, he felt obliged to give her fair warning that tonight, if she came to call again, she might discover a live tiger in his bed rather than a dead chicken.

'Oh, by the way,' he said in an attempt at nonchalance, 'you won't have to shake me awake in the morning like you did today. My tee-off time isn't till ten-thirty so I won't be knocking myself out with sleeping pills again tonight.' With that said, he felt it appropriate to change the subject. 'Do you really think there's any chance of my making the cut?'

For a while she did not answer. Instead she cast him a long and lingering look.

'You can do anything you set your mind to,' she said. 'Just remember that, Henry – *you can do anything at all.*'

After Charlie had turned off her light, Henry lay awake until the moon hoisted itself into the sky, higher, higher, until its beams again slanted down through the venetian blinds into the room. Over and over again, since he had first crawled into bed, he had asked himself whether Charlie would visit him again tonight, and, if so, what did he plan to do about it? What time it was when he fell asleep, he did not know. The next thing he was aware of was waking, instantly alert. Even before he directed his eyes across the room he sensed Charlie's approaching presence.

Like last night she glided towards him with a gleam in her eye that even the darkness could not hide. A flickering moonbeam palpitated before her step. Her golden hair shimmered on her shoulders. He caught his breath to appraise again the

149

perfection of her body. He knew now how Abu Ben Adam must have felt when startled awake by that visiting angel. As Charlie slowly approached, Henry continued to gaze at her, his eyes magnetized.

'Hello, Charlie,' he heard himself whisper.

Without answering she seated herself beside him and touched his lips with her fingers. When she leaned to kiss his brow, he felt the tips of her breasts graze his chest, warm and tingling, offering more excitement that he had ever experienced in his life.

Henry's devilish interior voice began speaking to him with more conviction than ever before ... *Ah, yes, Henry, she wants you, needs you . . . . Can't you understand that in the daytime she's simply too shy to let you know . . . . She's only pretending to be sleep-walking. That whole story is a ridiculous hoax. After years of frustration, old pal, you have a rendezvous with heaven. Keep it, Henry ... now.*

In the dim moonlight of the room Henry could not stop staring at one gorgeous pink nipple that quivered close to his face. In fact he felt himself growing cross-eyed as slowly, very slowly, he moved his lips towards its beckoning splendour. But even as he did so, he could not ignore the sound of that other interior voice now beginning to whisper a cautioning rebuttal ... *Come to your senses, Henry Summerfill! You've got to save your energy for tomorrow's second round. Do you really want to blow your chances for golfing immortality in return for a fleeting moment of sexual excitement? ... Hell, anyone can screw, but only sixty men in the whole world can make the cut at the Open! ... And suppose Charlie really is sleep-walking after all! Before making any advances, shouldn't you familiarize yourself with the Colorado penal code in regard to seducing a young woman prevented from exercising her free will because of being in a state of rhonbencephalic sleep or whatever? ... Furthermore, old boy, Martha is your woman, remember? Have you forgotten that 'forsaking all others' vow?...*

Suddenly, in a clear illuminating light, Henry Summerfill knew what had to be done! He could only live with his conscience after steering Charlie back to her own bed. At that point, if she made further physical overtures towards him, he would know what she was asking for without having to request it with words. But tempted as he might be, he vowed not to spend the rest of the night locked in such a variety of intricate embraces that they might have trouble figuring out how to disentangle themselves in time for tomorrow's tee off.

With no further procrastination, Henry put his plan into action. He rose quietly and steered Charlie by the elbow back through the doorway into her room. Once inside, he began groping in the darkness to place her back into bed. Without warning he tripped on an unseen paint can and lurched forward into his hostage. Together, in a clatter of spilling cans and protesting bedsprings, he tumbled on top of her.

'Oh my God!' she shouted. 'Henry, how *could* you!'

Before he could explain how it happened, his right eye was the recipient of an emphatic female fist.

24

The next afternoon Henry paced back and forth beside where his tee shot had come to rest in the sixteenth fairway. He and the two touring pros he was paired with, John Cook and Peter Jacobsen, were held up by the threesome ahead who in turn awaited the arrival of a USGA official at the green to rule on some questionable situation. It seemed to Henry that the USGA rules were more complex than the myriad regulations set forth by the Securities Exchange Commission which he was forced to deal with in his now all but forgotten business life.

Henry wished things would get moving ahead – his need to relieve his bladder was growing more urgent with every passing minute. When he glanced up towards the television tower behind the sixteenth green he made sure his sports shirt was neatly tucked into the waist of the hip hugging Madras slacks he was wearing for the first time. It was only after he had begun his round of golf that he had grown uncomfortably aware that the slacks must have been designed for a figure far slimmer than his own. But his primary concern as to his appearance was physical rather than sartorial; his swollen right eye was fast changing hue from crimson to purple to black. Charlie Bottomley, on discovering what she had done, had all but wept in apology after Henry explained he had simply been escorting her discreetly back to her bed. Now if one of those television cameras zoomed in on his disfigured eye, with what excuse could he plead his innocence to a domestic audience of 30 million viewers and, more important perhaps, to Martha who just might pick up the telecast in Naples? Nor was it too far-fetched to assume that he might be one of today's contestants selected for a quickie appearance on the tube. Despite his shooting two double-bogeys he had also sunk some phenomenal birdie-putts and now stood at only one over par for the day after fifteen holes. And from the news he had picked up from around the course, that was pretty damn good – especially with the greens now lightning-fast after having dried out by yesterday's strong winds. Apparently only Henry, with his magically sensitized Top-Flite, was able to avoid disaster on the greens. While Cook and Jacobson stared in amazement, Henry's putts too often ended up in the bottom of the cup as if pulled there by an invisible thread.

Now as he waited on the sixteenth fairway he felt an increasing need to rid himself of the two jumbo iced teas he had recently drunk. But here at the Open that situation was not so readily resolved as it would be if he were playing with his buddies back at Rolling Hills. There the nearest tree served splendidly as an *ad hoc* privy. By contrast, here at Spruce Valley not only were there dozens of strategically located cameras capable of zooming in at the unzipping of a fly but there were spectators present in every direction, large groups stationed around the greens and even larger throngs following the play of the top golfing luminaries.

The largest such crowd on the course was now approaching from the opposite direction down an adjacent fairway. While Henry was gazing towards the swarm of people, wondering whom they might be following, he spotted a Kilroy's Kastle all but hidden in a cluster of pines. It was one of the portable chemical toilets which, for the convenience of spectators, were placed around the course. Again Henry appraised the delay-of-game situation at the sixteenth green just ahead, then hurried towards the cabin and stepped inside the squeaky metal door.

A few seconds later, as he was set to leave, he noticed that the laces on one of his shoes had come untied. When he hurriedly leaned over to remedy the matter he heard a severe ripping of cloth. With nervous, enquiring fingers he was then appalled to discover he had torn out the entire seat of his too-tight Madras slacks.

He told himself not to panic. Unless he could think of an immediate solution, he would still be trapped inside his metal cabin when it was his turn to resume play, thus drawing an immediate disqualification. Then, fortunately, he remembered that the pants to his rain gear were in the big pocket of his golf bag. By inconspicuously making his way back to his caddy, he could slip his rain pants over his torn Madras slacks and finish the round, perhaps not in the height of fashion, but at least without subjecting himself to possible arrest for indecent exposure.

When Henry turned the door handle it emitted a loud, protesting squeak. Then he stood in the open doorway, his eyes large as wagon wheels. Not more than twenty feet ahead, surrounded by a monstrous gallery, Greg Norman, apparently having hit a wayward drive from the adjacent hole, was just addressing the ball for his recovery shot from the trees. At the squeaking sound behind him, the Shark slowly turned his head. Along with his horde of followers he stared curiously into Henry's face.

With a mutter of apology Henry took a quick step back

inside the latrine and slammed its door shut. He leaned against the inside wall, breathing fast, colour flooding his face, waiting for the sound of Norman's shot so that the crowd would disappear, allowing Henry to make his exit. But instead of hearing a club-face contacting a golf ball, he was startled by a knock on the door.

'Say, fella, why don't you come out?'

Henry recognized the voice as belonging to none other than Greg Norman himself.

'I don't mean to bug you but I can't concentrate on my shot knowing you're in there. How do I know you're not going to squeak the door again just at the top of my backswing? You'd really be doing me a favour if you'd come out right now.'

Henry hesitated, then placed his lips to the crack of the door. '*Pssst – there's no seat left in my pants. I promise I'll stay very still so that . . . .*'

The metal door jangled from a heavy drumroll of knocking.

'Hey, you inside, this is a USGA official speaking. Do you realize you're holding up this whole goddamn tournament? Mr Norman would prefer you to be out of there before he continues play.'

Henry saw the door being pulled open and found himself face to face with an official thrusting forward his bulldog jaw. Just past the man's shoulder stood the Shark grinning apologetically. Beyond, as far as Henry could see, all of humanity seemed to be staring into his face. He took a deep breath, said a quick prayer, and attempted to shield his rear with both hands. The crowd cheered as he stepped from the latrine doorway. Keeping his back to the gallery as best he could, he slithered sideways towards his own fairway, his eyes still defensively aimed at the sea of grinning faces pointed his way.

155

25

At ten o'clock that night Katie Summerfill raced through Gate 16 at the airport terminal in Denver and leaped into her father's arms.

'You made the cut, you made the cut! I couldn't be more excited!' She disengaged herself from his arms long enough to step back and proudly appraise him. But her smile gave way to a gasp.... 'Daddy! Where did you get that awful black eye?'

Henry had already rehearsed his answer.

'Just a stupid mistake, honey. I was doing one of my isometric exercises – the one where my hands have a tug-of-war with each other – and I somehow lost my grip and hit myself in the eye.'

He quickly chose to shift the conversation to golf as they moved towards the baggage-claim area. 'Like I told you when I phoned, my putts just dropped in from everywhere. I'm only four strokes off the lead.' He felt as though he was floating rather than walking, but he also felt due for an awful crash. 'It's like some crazy dream, Katie. Guess how many players have thirty-six-hole scores better than mine? Only *thirteen!*' His chin quivered ever so slightly. 'I'm getting nervous about tomorrow, Katie – I mean, *really* nervous.' He plucked his daughter's suitcase from the baggage carousel. They headed for the car park. 'We play in twosomes for the final two days,' he told her. 'Guess who I tee off with at twelve-twenty tomorrow?'

'Who?'

'Nick Faldo. Can you believe that, Katie – *Nick Faldo!*'

'Wow.'

'What if I make a complete fool of myself?'

'Now listen,' she ordered, 'stop psyching yourself out that way. You're one of only sixty-two golfers left in the tournament. And the only amateur. You're still in it because you scored better than those who didn't make the cut. Am I right?'

'Well, yes but—'

'No buts, no ifs, no maybes. Don't you dare even so much as whisper to yourself that you can't win. You've got to believe with all your heart that you not only can but will. The world of achievement belongs to the optimist and don't you forget it.'

As they drove through the night towards Shadow Mountain Lodge, Henry found himself trying not to answer directly Katie's questions about Charlie Bottomley.

'Did she walk in her sleep again last night?' Katie was asking.

Henry hesitated. 'Only briefly .... Oh, say, have you noticed whether we're still on Interstate Seventy?'

'Did she come to your bed, Daddy?'

'Katie, I asked you whether—'

'Yes, Daddy, we're still on Interstate Seventy. Did Charlie come to your bed again last night?'

'Look, honey, she's moved to the Holiday Inn. It's not important any more.'

'I know it's not important. But it *is* intriguing. However, I agree we shouldn't discuss it any more. There's golf to be played. And a tournament to be won.'

For Henry, forgetting Charlie was easier said than done. To think that she had twice come to his bedside, and he had not even touched her. Now, of course, he never would. Even though he recognized the naïvety of his new-found obsession – that of nestling one of her perfect breasts in his hand – perhaps fate had deemed it wisest that such a momentous occasion should never occur. If perchance he were ever to explore that tantalizing territory his internal chemistry might react very much as if he had been struck by lightning.

At the next exit he turned off the main highway on to the narrow winding road that climbed through the foothills towards Shadow Mountain Lodge. Could it be that he allowed his thoughts to wander off on such sensual bypaths simply as a defence mechanism against facing up to the secret advantage he held over every other Open contestant? Now the thought of it closed in on him again, mushrooming in his conscience.

'Oh, Katie,' he burst out finally, 'I feel so rotten about play-ing with these phony balls. I know you keep insisting they don't violate any regulations but I'll tell you this – I couldn't break a hundred on this course with an ordinary ball. I don't know if it's my nervousness or my guilt complex but I'm not sure I'll even be able to stand up on the first tee tomorrow, let alone swing the club.'

'You'll make it all right,' Katie assured him as they pulled up to the motel. 'Before the time comes for us to leave for the golf-course in the morning, you and I are going to have a very special sort of session.'

The next morning Henry's eyes followed Katie sceptically as she moved to the window of the motel room and pulled shut the blinds against the sun.

'Are you sure you know what you're doing?' he asked from the straight chair she had seated him in.

'Place both feet flat on the floor,' she instructed, 'and rest your hands in your lap, palms up . . . . There, that's good.'

Earlier, he had introduced Katie to Charlie Bottomley at breakfast, and the two of them had hit it off surprisingly well. But a few minutes ago Katie had politely excused Charlie from their presence and now circled the chair on which her father sat.

'Is there any chance you'll hypnotize me *too* completely?' he asked. 'I've got to be more alert today than ever in my life.'

'You're not only going to be alert, Daddy, but wonderfully relaxed and confident as well.' She removed the telephone from its cradle and stuffed it beneath a pillow in a dressing-table drawer. She returned to face him, speaking serenely but distinctly in the dimness of the room.

'There's no reason for nervousness, Daddy – no reason at all. You'll find this to be very pleasant, very soothing.' She stepped through the doorway into her room just long enough to retrieve a shiny Top-Flite attached to an all but invisible thread. She lifted it until the golf ball hung perhaps eighteen inches in front of his eyes.

'All right, Daddy, you are now going to disregard your surroundings and pay attention to everything I say. Just keep your eyes on this ball as it now begins to swing to and fro ... to and fro ... to and fro . . . . Breathe in slowly, deeply . . . . Good . . . Now exhale, slowly, fully . . . . Oh, that's *very* good! ... Now each time you exhale I want you to start calmly counting aloud, backwards from ninety-nine . . . .'

Henry felt his eyelids begin to grow heavy as he kept staring at the ball . . . . 'Ninety-nine ...' He took another slow deep breath, then eased it out again . . . . 'Ninety-eight . . . .'

By the time he had counted down to ninety-four, the ball

159

grew fuzzy before his eyes and his body seemed to lose contact with the chair. After he had reached eighty-seven his mouth formed the words but his voice had grown still. At eighty-one his lips barely moved and he could no longer hold his eyes open.

His daughter's voice, soft and slow, seemed to come from a great distance, telling him that he was transported on to a cloud ... falling ... rising ... drifting .... His normal consciousness, she advised him, had sunk beneath the surface of his mind but his awareness remained poised to relay messages to his subconscious.

'You, Henry Summerfill, are now blissfully relaxed and untroubled. No matter what might happen on the golf-course today you will face it with an easy confidence unlike anything you have ever experienced before.' The voice seemed to move even further away, yet each word echoed inside him with the clarity of a bell .... 'I want you to imprint on your motor reflexes exactly how your golf swing feels when you hit your most beautiful shots. Concentrate on that strong harmonious feeling .... Throughout today's round you will instinctively reconstruct and repeat, time after time, that identical marvellous blending of mind and muscle and nerve ... You will be surrounded by crowds of people and television cameras but nothing will distract you from playing with superlative confidence ....'

Each of his daughter's words swirled deliciously into the very core of his awareness and he believed it all without question or doubt .... *Never forget that what the mind of man can conceive and believe, it can achieve. Yes, Henry Summerfill, today you are going to shoot the greatest round of golf of your life ....*'

160

26

Henry stood at the fringe of the twelfth green and watched Nick Faldo blast out of the sand-trap to within twenty inches of the hole. The stroke was so masterfully authoritative and so poetic in its execution that Henry could not help but join the sizeable gallery in applauding the shot. It was only after he had stopped clapping that it dawned on him that contestants were expected to refrain from such displays of mutual admiration. And yet the true enigma of their round through the first eleven holes was that Henry, because of his miraculous putting, together with the fact he couldn't hit the ball far enough to find trouble, remained level with Faldo at one under for the day.

Henry couldn't get over how effectively Katie's hypnotic spell was working. Despite the embarrassment of his black eye, he had remained relaxed and free, chatting amicably with Faldo as if they had become the closest of buddies. Occasionally, when Henry caught a glimpse of his daughter in the crowd, she would beam back at him with excitement. But Charlie Bottomley, true to her pledge not to hex him with her presence, was nowhere in sight. That was calming to Henry, especially after having witnessed earlier the scoop-necked polka-dot blouse she had chosen to wear. She would be waiting for him in the crowd, she had promised, when he reached the final green. To Henry that was something to look forward to. By then his need to concentrate solely on golf for the day would be ended.

After Faldo had marked his ball following his remarkable sand-shot at the twelfth hole Henry studied the roll of the green, then crouched down over his stubby putter and tapped the ball towards the hole thirty feet away. The crowd gasped in amazement – and Faldo's eyes again all but bugged out – as Henry's birdie-putt seemed to break first to the right and then to the left before diving into the hole with the speed of a frightened chipmunk.

On the par-five thirteenth, Henry reached the green with a drive, a three-wood and a four-iron, all undramatically steady. In contrast, Faldo traversed the same 520-yard distance in only two shots, each so astounding in power and beauty that Henry could not refrain from crying aloud in amazement. Unfortunately for the British player, however, a sudden strong gust of wind veered his second shot off course at the last instant, sending the ball skidding on to a bare mound just off the green.

Faldo was addressing his third shot when another surprising gust of wind swept across the playing area. To Henry's surprise, he then observed his playing mate hesitate and step back from the ball, beckoning a nearby USGA official. When Faldo and the official put their heads together in conference, a hideous thought crossed Henry's mind: could it be that Nick was suggesting launching an official inquiry into what the hell was going on regarding so many of Summerfill's erratic putts ending up in the hole? But Henry soon learned otherwise. When the wind gusted, Faldo's ball had been nudged by the wind perhaps one-eighth of an inch after Nick had taken his stance. As a consequence, Faldo had felt it his

162

duty to call a penalty stroke on himself in keeping with the uncompromising USGA rulebook. To Henry it seemed completely unfair. Had Faldo not voluntarily penalized himself, no one would have known the ball had slightly shifted its position.

Suddenly Henry's latent feelings of guilt about his doctored Top-Flites burst the bubble of his hypnotic spell. His knees began to shake, his skin began to crawl and his palms grew so clammy he was forced to wipe them on his trouser-leg before selecting his club for his tee-shot on the short but perilous fourteenth hole. No longer did he feel himself to be a veritable Adonis of a man with twenty-twenty vision and not a single protesting muscle in his body. His Cinderella existence had ceased – he was back again to the Henry D. Summerfill of old; a middle-aged bumbling incompetent golfer, now sporting an ugly black eye, surrounded by thousands of spectators, spied upon by soaring television platforms and, from higher still, by the MetLife blimp that he had waved up to now and then while playing the earlier holes.

He tried to shake away the fear that had enveloped him as he gazed towards the fourteenth flag 160 yards away, the green being guarded in front by the rushing, boulder-strewn waters of Cherokee Creek. Striking a final note of terror to his heart were the three yawning sand-traps protecting the small green, and the out-of-bounds fence just beyond. The longer Henry stared at the scene after addressing the ball, the more tense he grew, and when he finally backed away from the shot he could sense the bewilderment of the crowd. From a corner of his eye he caught sight of Katie casting him a pleading look of encouragement.

Again he addressed the ball, his eyes fearfully wandering to the rushing waters of Cherokee Creek which cut its swath across the fairway just in front of the green. This was no shot for the faint of heart. For the first time since the tournament had begun he picked up the whisperings of his evil interior voice . . . . *Well, Henry, nothing can save you now ... neither your daughter's hypnotic spell nor those doctored-up golf balls! You can't even remember how to swing, can you? If you're able to hit the ball at all, you're going to send it right smack into the jaws of the creek. Come on, goddammit, don't just stand there with the shakes — you're holding up play. Just swing the club and accept your fate like a man . . . .*

Henry felt himself grow sicker. If this mutinous interior voice was destined to return to haunt him, why had it waited till now, for God's sake, when the eyes of the whole world were watching?

Henry's club began its fateful swing. Instead of the slow smooth arc he had enjoyed up until this moment, his club slashed ungracefully through the thin Colorado air, propelling itself awkwardly downwards. He raised his head and shoulders prematurely, barely catching the upper half of the ball with the club-face. His Top-Flite dived forward, just as his evil voice had predicted, heading towards the turbulent creek. Henry dropped his eyes in shame. But when he heard an explosive roar from the crowd he jerked his head to see that his ball was safely across the water after apparently having bounded forward from a boulder in the middle of the creek. While Henry felt none too pleased that his shot had come to rest in a bunker, that was infinitely better than the fate he rightfully deserved.

A few minutes later, his nerves still frayed, he struck his sand-shot poorly, again catching only the upper half of the ball. Instead of it lobbing softly towards the hole, it took off in high gear as if shot from a rifle, heading out of bounds past the green. But as his ball sped past the pin, still gaining altitude, it entangled itself in the flag, vanishing from sight as the square of yellow cloth convulsed with pain. After what seemed an eternity it disgorged the ball straight down the flag stick into the hole. Along with hundreds of spectators, Henry stared in stunned silence. His two worst shots of the tournament had occurred one after the other – and they had provided him with a birdie-two, now moving him three stokes under par for the day.

When Henry stepped to the next tee he felt neither relaxed nor tense, neither strong nor weak – just utterly numb. Could what was happening be for real – or was this entire adventure just an unbelievable dream? From the fifteenth to the seventeenth holes, he watched his drives ricochet off trees to bound back on to the fairway. On the sixteenth, he shanked his approach shot, the ball skidding away from his club-face at a right angle. After cracking into a spectator's camera it careered safely back into play, allowing him to salvage par.

Twenty minutes later, in the television tower behind the eighteenth green, NBC's Dick Enberg and Johnny Miller were describing to more than 40 million viewers the scene now unfolding:

'This,' said Enberg, his voice growing with excitement, 'is a most remarkable turn of events. From out of total obscurity has emerged amateur Henry Summerfill who – should it be his good fortune to birdie this eighteenth hole – can wrest the lead from Tom Lehman with only one day of play remaining. And if, by chance, Summerfill could hold on to the lead through tomorrow's final round, he would become the first amateur to win this prestigious United States Open since Johnny Goodman turned the trick sixty-five years ago. Our roving commentator, Gary Koch, has been following the twosome of Summerfill and Faldo for the past three holes. Come in, Gary, will you, and give us your close-up impression of what's going on . . . .'

'Thanks, Dick. What we're seeing today is an absolute phenomenon. First off, Summerfill is built a little differently from your ordinary tournament golfer ... and his swing is certainly unique ... but you can't argue with success. Despite the fact that he doesn't hit the ball nearly as far as Faldo – and has now begun to hit it very poorly, actually – his putting is so deadly that, well, to be honest about it, he's the only player on the course who seems to have worked out how to conquer these undulating lightning-fast greens.... But now the crowd has quieted down because Summerfill is about to hit his approach shot into the eighteenth green. All right, now he's addressing the ball.... There's his swing ... the shot is on its way, but, oh-oh, I'm afraid he's hit it too low and too strong. It's racing quail-high past the pin and ... wow! There it goes into the crowd behind the green! Oh, I do hope no one got hurt. Johnny Miller, you're right there in the tower above where it happened. Back to you....'

'Yes, thank you Gary.... I think Summerfill's ball may have hit a woman's handbag or some other object. I say that because the ball leaped straight up, seeming to hang in the air for a moment, then dropping back into the crowd. Now some marshals are hurrying to find out where the ball has come to rest, presumably just behind the green. And that's going to be a monster of a shot for Summerfill. There's no way, I'd wager, that he could possibly birdie the hole. Chances are that he won't even be able to salvage his par because, from that direc- tion, the green is downhill and slick as ice. We'll be back in one minute after the break....'

When the telecast of the tournament resumed, Roger Maltbie, covering the activity on the eighteenth green for NBC, reported on a most unusual and rather ticklish turn of events – Summerfill's ball, which, surprisingly, could not be discovered for some time, had at last been reported found, but not on the playing surface of the course. It had instead dropped into the depths of a shapely young blonde's polka-dot blouse. Five minutes later the officials were still huddled in an argument, now and then turning to consult with Henry Summerfill and with the voluptuous young spectator who still sheltered the ball precisely where it had come to rest . . . .

'Roger, you're on the spot. Can you tell us what the delay is all about?'

'It's an interpretation of one of the very cumbersome USGA rules that the officials have run up against,' explained Maltbie. 'In this case the applicable provision is section one of rule nineteen which pertains to a ball becoming lodged on or in what has technically been interpreted as, well ... *as an outside moveable agency!* With that determination now resolved Summerfill will of course be afforded a free drop. But now the officials are trying to reach agreement on Rule Twenty which has to do with who should rescue the ball from its present, shall we say, non-playable lie . . . .'

While the officials continued huddling, the television cameras picked up some brief action on other holes, then returned to Dick Enberg in the tower above the eighteenth green.

'We have just been advised,' he said, 'of the ruling. Henry Summerfill may elect to retrieve the ball himself or, fortunately, he may designate another individual to do so. That means the young lady – who incidentally is wearing a reporter's badge marked Bottomley – may personally perform the task, freeing Summerfill from what surely would be a most ticklish circumstance . . . . Despite that option Henry Summerfill seems to be blushing rather furiously as he continues his nervous pacing to and fro. In the tower here we are first-hand witnesses to these rather unusual proceedings because both Sommerfill and this absolutely smashing young

woman are immediately below us, offering us a most exceptional vantage point to witness this forthcoming bit of golfing
byplay .... What's this? Oh, this is hard to believe – Henry
Summerfill has advised the officials that he will personally
fetch the ball from its present hidden location .... As you
might suspect, the marshals are having trouble holding back
the crowd – everyone seems crazy to witness Summerfill's
next move .... Well, there he goes, sports fans. The colour of
his face is fast turning from red to purple. Now his fingertips
are creeping into the young woman's rather open-necked
blouse ... now his hand is disappearing .... Oh Lord, now
not even his wrist is visible. Strangely enough she seems to be
smiling .... *Hold on! Something seems to be the matter. I think his
hand has got caught. Perhaps he's simply trying to – my God, what
is he trying to do? ... Actually, the more he fumbles the more she
titters – oops, sorry about that! ... Ah, success at last. Summerfill
has retrieved the ball. But wait! – something is wrong with him –
he's just standing there dazed, or as if struck by lightning.*

'All right,' continued Enberg, a long moment later,
'Summerfill finally seems to be regaining some notion of time
and place. Now he has taken his drop and is going to putt the
ball from just off the back fringe of the green. Yes, folks, that
implement trembling in his hands that looks like a hammer is
actually his putter. As we mentioned earlier, we haven't seen
a single player get anywhere near the hole on this extremely
fast downhill curving shot .... All right, Summerfill is
crouching down into his somewhat grotesque putting
stance .... Now here comes his putt down this sharply sloping green. Just as I feared, he's hit it much too hard. Poor
chap! – that ball might even wind up in the bunker below the
green. What's more, he's woefully misjudged the break – his
ball is curving away from the hole to the right .... Or is it? ...
Suddenly it's curving the other way and – this is incredible! –

the ball seems to be slowing down, almost as if it had brakes. *it's – it's – my God – it's – yes – it's in the hole!* ... With that unbelievable birdie-putt, Henry Summerfill has just leaped into the third-round lead of the US Open. The marshals are having a hard time keeping the crowd away from him. But something seems definitely wrong with Summerfill. He's stunned – absolutely immobilized there at the fringe of the green . . . .

What's this? The young lady in the polka-dot blouse is ducking under ropes. Two security guards have caught her . . . . No, she's broken free again – she's hurling herself into Henry Summerfill's arms . . . . Now she's smothering him with kisses . . . . The crowd is cheering and the bloody television cameras are zooming in for close-ups . . . . Never in all of sporting history, my friends, has there been such an absolutely devastating moment as this!'

27

Nearly half an hour elapsed after Henry finished his round before he felt himself returning to the world of reality. Only in the vaguest way could he recall that a cordon of security guards had disentangled him from Charlie Bottomley's embrace and that Nick Faldo had then benevolently shepherded him into the scorer's tent, where Henry signed his card and handed it to the scoring committee.

What, Henry asked himself, had happened next? As far as he could remember, several of the touring pros had stared at him as if he were some sort of freak. And hadn't Johnny Miller then interviewed him on television, questioning him unmercifully, it seemed, as to why he had taken so long to extract his golf ball from inside the young woman's apparel? And was it for real or had he only imagined that NBC had kept replaying stop-action television clips of his adventure inside that low-cut blouse, seeking to substantiate that his search for the golf ball had been diverted by the attraction of a warmer, fuller globe? Henry could only hope that the tournament was not being beamed by satellite into Portofino where his wife was presently ensconced.

Now, as Henry became more aware of his immediate surroundings, he realized that a circle of reporters and well-wishers kept crowding in, asking questions that he heard himself answering only after guidance from a small counselling voice close at hand. The voice was that of his daughter, Katie.

'Almost all the top contenders have finished the third round now,' a reporter was saying, 'and you're still number one on the leader board. Do you feel that tomorrow you'll be the first amateur since 1933 to win the US Open?' The reporter's eyes widened as his gaze shifted from Henry's face to past his shoulder. And when Henry felt his daughter's hand fearfully clutch his own, he turned to find himself confronted by three grim-faced USGA officials who had charged their way through the tightly packed throng. The crowd fell ominously silent.

One of the blue-blazered officials, identified by his badge as Mr Cain, stepped even closer and removed the pipe from between his clenched teeth.

'Mr Summerfill, it has come to light that you are guilty – flagrantly guilty, I'm sorry to say – of violating section 6B of USGA rule six. It is therefore my regrettable duty to advise you that you are disqualified from further play in this tournament.'

Henry felt the world collapse around him. And his evil interior voice wasted no time in leaping to the fore . . . . *Aha, they found out about your Top-Flites, didn't they? Hell, it was bound to happen, especially after that flukey snake you sunk on the eighteenth hole with the cameras grinding and all those spectators watching* . . . .

Shameful as it was, Henry was more than ready to purge his guilt. He was seeking the proper words of confession when his daughter stepped between him and the officials.

'As of now,' said Katie to Mr Cain, 'you have yet to recite what that rule states.'

'In short, little girl, your father failed to sign his scorecard properly.'

Henry could only gasp in disbelief. On the one hand, he was stunned by the accusation – he distinctly remembered signing his card as required in the scorer's tent. On the other hand, his relief could not have been greater that his disqualification had not been prompted by the discovery of something peculiar about his golf balls. Henry heard his own voice as if from afar.

'I know I took my card from Nick Faldo and signed it.'

The official remained stony-faced as he thrust the scorecard under Henry's nose.

'Now tell me does that signature read: Henry Summerfill?'

Henry's mouth fell open. The card was signed: *Boobs Bottomley.*

'I – I don't understand it,' he cried. 'I guess I just, I just –' Henry's voice fell off helplessly.

'In his confusion he simply signed another name,' interjected Katie. 'Really, you can't be serious about disqualifying my father on such a ridiculous technicality as that! Thirty million TV viewers know that it was my father and not, well, not Ms Bottomley who shot that score.'

'Incidentally,' barked the official, 'just who the hell *is* this – this – this Bottomley?'

Henry tried pulling himself together.

'She's that – that moveable outside agency who trapped my ball.'

'But why,' demanded Mr Cain, 'would she be signing your scorecard?'

'She didn't sign my card,' Henry managed. 'Like I said a moment ago, this odd trance came over me and I . . . .'

'Wouldn't everything be solved,' Katie interjected, 'if Daddy simply signed his own name right now?'

Another of the officials wasted no time in opening the USGA rules of golf.

'Sub-section C of section six of rule six reads as follows: *No alteration may be made on a card after the competitor has returned it to the Committee.*' He removed his pipe from his mouth and endeavoured to bless Katie with a compassionate smile. 'Your father has already turned in his card. Believe me, the same penalty would have been imposed on Jack Nicklaus if he had signed his name Peter Rabbit. What are rules for if not to be abided by?'

The crowd, which had now grown even larger in size, awaited the rebuttal.

'Rules are designed to protect the innocent,' answered Katie, 'not to persecute them.'

As Henry listened to his fate being argued, he resented, as a matter of principle, that the USGA refused to acknowledge officially that he had shot his superlative round. But as a matter of another even stronger principle he knew he was guilty of grossly unfair tactics in having played with a doctored golf ball. Yet whenever he tried to withdraw voluntarily from the tournament in accordance with the wishes of the three USGA officials, Katie interceded with arguments as to why the ruling concerning his scorecard made no sense whatsoever. And the more she argued, the more the spectators shouted their encouragement and the more the USGA officials cast one another nervous glances.

'The rule in question,' she said, 'states that a player must attest to his score by signing his card, right?'

'Right,' said Mr Cain.

'I contend that my father did just that. True, because he was preoccupied, he signed the name of another individual but it was *he* who affixed the name to the card as required, right?'

'That sounds fair,' piped up an interested bystander. A

wave of agreement swept through the tightly packed throng.

The officials bit on their pipestems nervously.

'I have a feeling,' mumbled Mr Cain to his cohorts, 'that this little girl is trying to back us into a corner.'

'I think we're already in the corner,' one of his colleagues replied behind the back of his hand.

'I will now convince you beyond a shadow of doubt,' said Katie, 'that my father's own hand wrote out the words – if you'll pardon my saying them – Boobs Bottomley, on this scorecard in question.'

'Come on, Katie,' whispered Henry, emerging slowly from his trance, 'let's just forget the whole thing and get out of here.'

But Katie ignored his plea. Instead she heard the crowd egging her on.

'As you gentlemen no doubt know,' she said, 'graphological analysis is a psycho-diagnostic aid in establishing error-free criteria for an objective evaluation of handwriting identification.' She reached out and took the scorecard from the fingers of Mr Cain. Next, after making her father sign his name below his previous signing, Katie displayed the card to the growing crush of spectators.

'While there are literally dozens of elements that separate one person's writing style from anyone else's, simply by symbolically interpreting the constancy patterns of only a few of these elements we can readily substantiate that these two signatures on the scorecard were written by one and the same person ... my father.'

'Look, little girl,' said Mr Cain, 'this is—'

'Will you please stop calling me "little girl".'

Mr Cain squeezed his pipestem until his knuckles turned white.

'This is a golf tournament,' he said as calmly as possible,

'not a courtroom. So stop groping for extenuating circumstances. The USGA Rules Committee has already—'

A chorus of boos drowned out his next words.

'I will ask you now to please compare,' continued Katie, 'the fullness of all the signature strokes, the slightly leftward slant of the vertical stems, the inflated upper loops of the corresponding h's and l's, the stroke and placement of the i dots.' When a cameraman from *Sports Illustrated* aimed his lens at the scorecard, Katie held it very still for the benefit of that magazine's millions of subscribers. 'Note too,' she went on, 'the same originality in the form levels and the domain of instinct in both the upper and lower zones . . . . yes, both signatures were affixed to this scorecard by my father, Henry Summerfill, who is now about to be officially reinstated for play in tomorrow's final round of this tournament, right?'

'Right,' chanted the crowd in unison.

The three USGA officials fearfully scanned the sea of faces around them. They glanced mutely at one another, then down into Katie's face.

'Right,' they whispered together.

28

'You shouldn't have pressed the matter, Katie. Those officials offered me a perfect excuse for getting off the hook. You know I have no right to be leading this tournament, or, for that matter, even to be competing here.' Henry could not keep the disillusionment from his voice as he sat behind the wheel of their car in the parking lot of the Spruce Valley Country Club. After having eluded the press, he and Katie had hopped into the car to make a quick getaway only to find that they were blocked by other cars parked both in front and behind. Henry slid lower in the seat so as not to be spotted. He hated being a celebrity. How could he have held such false day-dreams of glory for so many years? 'I just can't go through with it,' he muttered.

All the while that he had been remonstrating with himself, his daughter had been thumbing the pages of the USGA rule-book that he had left in the car. When she found Appendix III, headed *The Ball*, she read it to him, slowly and clearly, in an effort to set his mind at ease once more. The Top-Flites she had prepared for him in no way violated a single requirement specified in the rule. And again she reminded him that all the golf manufacturers and the top pros of the game were constantly seeking legitimate ways to improve the performance of their equipment.

'You've got to get over your guilt complex, Daddy. You're just naturally nervous because you're the golfer out in front. Who wouldn't be nervous? After all, the US Open is something special. Sacred almost.'

'That's my point, Katie. It *is* sacred. And damn it, right now I feel sacrilegious as hell.' He stared blankly out over the parking lot as he recalled that day in April when he descended the basement stairs at home where Katie in her laboratory had been using one of his golf balls as a part of her experiment for the forthcoming Junior Science Fair. Yes, he had been the culprit in wanting to try that golf ball out under regular playing conditions. She had protested but he had begged and pouted until she had accompanied him to the Rolling Hills course where, with only her to see him, he had teed-up that one-of-a-kind Top-Flite and set it flying down the first fairway.

'I certainly didn't ever intend for things to lead to this,' he said aloud. 'I only wanted to be able to hit my tee shots as far as Alex Wulf.'

'But, Daddy, it's not the ball alone that has made all that difference in your game. You're swinging a lot better now because you're no longer tempted to try to kill the ball. You're getting respectable distance with a nice smooth swing.'

'But that doesn't account for what's happening to me on the greens. If you hadn't given the ball those properties of – of—'

'Oscillatory rejection, Daddy.'

'Yes, well, without that I'd never get a single putt in the hole. All the pros are saying that these are the toughest greens to putt they've ever encountered.'

'You're just too modest about your own ability,' Katie said. 'Don't you suppose it might be your new putting technique that mostly makes the difference?'

'I'd like to believe that, Katie, but I just can't. And deep down in your heart you know that what you've done to alter the ball is one hundred per cent responsible for all that's happened to me.' Henry felt a new strength of character seeping into him. Always before when he and Katie had discussed the matter, he had let her convince him that everything was on the up and up. 'I have something to say to you, Katie. And, please, no interruptions.'

He reached across the car seat and took her hand in his. 'I'm not going to argue with you any longer as to whether or not the Top-Flites I've been playing with conform to USGA requirements. Maybe they do, maybe they don't. If the matter resolved itself into a strictly legal issue, perhaps I'd be adjudged innocent of any technical violation.' Henry frowned, then spoke more slowly. 'But the fact that I may not have violated the letter of the law doesn't mean that I haven't violated the spirit of the law. I'm as guilty as can be, Katie, in having not been true to man's basic code of ethics. No amount of rationalization can absolve me from knowing I've not played the game fair and square. Worst of all, Katie, is that I'm setting one helluva poor example for my one and only daughter whom I love very much.' He squeezed her hand tighter. 'I was the instigator of it all. You went along with it and then got swept up in the excitement the same as I did. And neither of us – especially me – had the guts or the clearness of mind to blow the whistle on something we both pretended was right but knew was wrong.'

They sat together in silence.

'What do you plan to do?' Katie finally asked.

'I guess I'll just have to tell those USGA officials the truth and disqualify myself from further play.' He dropped his head and winced. 'That's why it would have been far less

178

humiliating for me to have been disqualified because of signing the scorecard wrong.'

Katie put her hand on his arm. 'I'm proud of you, Daddy, really proud. And I'll not try to argue you out of withdrawing. But don't you realize how much you could harm the game of golf if you revealed the truth?'

'What do you mean?'

'Just that you could ruin the game for good, that's all. If you let it be known that it has become scientifically possible to alter the reaction of golf balls in such a radical manner, every golf-ball manufacturer in the country would immediately set out to accomplish the same thing, and sooner or later they'd fit together the right pieces to solve the puzzle. That means that while still keeping the golf ball in compliance with the rules, suddenly everyone could get a longer roll on the ball and sink impossible putts from all over the green. Every golf-course in the world would become obsolete because it would play too easy. There would be no sport and excitement left in the game. Fantastic as it sounds, Daddy, those are the implications of what could happen if you go through with your confession.'

The longer Henry thought it over, the more he realized he would be damned if he did and damned if he didn't. He could think of no good course of action to take short of setting out purposely to break an arm or a leg prior to tomorrow's final round.

'What's your suggestion, Katie?'

'I don't think you have any choice but to finish the tournament,' she said. 'But if you truly feel it would be against your principles to win – or even to finish near the top – couldn't you just accidentally on purpose run up your score tomorrow? You know, like hitting some balls out of bounds and into water hazards and things like that.'

179

Henry sighed heavily. 'I hit several balls today that should have either gone out of bounds or ended up in Cherokee Creek. But you saw what happened. They sheered off trees or off portable outhouses or off spectators' kneecaps, all of them bouncing back into play. No, Katie, I just couldn't be sure that the same sort of insane luck wouldn't happen to me tomorrow.' He had no sooner finished his sentence when Charlie Bottomley appeared breathless beside his car window.

'I've been looking everywhere for you . . . . Oh, Henry, you poor mixed up baby! I hear that you signed my name – well, sort of – to your score card and almost got kicked out of the tournament. That's both so sad and so sweet I can hardly stand it.'

Even in Henry's preoccupied state he couldn't help but notice that Charlie still breathed heavily from having raced around in search of them. Strangely though, now that he had delved into that treasure chest – now that his fantasy had actually been realized, he surprised himself in this moment of stress by now wishing instead for his wife Martha's more comfortable, reassuring company.

Charlie clambered into the back seat of the car.

'Why were you so terribly nervous about retrieving the golf ball? It seemed that you kept getting mixed-up as to what you were looking for.'

Henry felt the tip of the ears turn pink. The implication of Charlie's words was hardly the sort of thing he wanted his twelve-year-old daughter to overhear.

'And I hope I didn't embarrass you when I gave you that little kiss on the eighteenth green.'

Katie rolled her eyes. 'That was a *little* kiss?'

'Well, I just couldn't help myself – it was all so exciting.' Charlie seemed beside herself with joy. 'This has got to be the luckiest day of my life. Here I've got all this story material on you, Henry, and I've got all these unusual pictures, and, well, this could prove to be my real breakthrough as a sports reporter. CBS might even want me for the next Olympic Games. Really, I . . . .'

Now that Charlie was out of view in the back seat, Henry's thoughts flooded back to the issue in hand – that of disqualifying himself from the tournament, even if it meant a confession of the truth. As Charlie and Katie rehashed the events of the day, Henry picked up the USGA rule book, absently thumbing its pages while he tried to reach his decision on what he must do. How could he have let himself get into such a mess? How could he have been such a lover of the game of golf and yet given it such a slap in the face? He caught sight of his image in the rearview mirror and could not have been more displeased with what he saw. It was not a sincere image at all – not the image of the Henry Summerfill who up until two months ago had always tried to be a good father to Katie and a good husband to Martha. More than anything, that was the status he wanted to achieve once more. As soon as possible he would cut his hair and let it return to its natural greyer shade, and would no longer wonder whether ultra-hold hair spray was better to use than extra-hold or super-hold. Yes, and he would give up these inconvenient soft contacts and these trendy clothes and settle back into being his old self again.

As he slowly scanned the pages of the Rules of Golf, his mind turned back to other Opens that he had either read about or watched on television. Wasn't it Horace Rawlins who won the first US Open golf championship in 1895, getting a gold medal and $150.00 cash? From then till now, the list of luminaries was staggering: Francis Ouimet and Walter Hagan, Bobby Jones and Gene Sarazen, Byron Nelson and Ben Hogan, the last-named having fought back from a near-fatal motor accident a year earlier to win the 1950 Open. Then other new giants had taken over – Arnold Palmer shooting that incredible final round in 1960; Nicklaus winning his classic duel in Palmer's home territory in 1962; Ken Venturi's storybook come-back from obscurity, stumbling with heat prostration with a doctor at his side to win at Congressional in 1964.

Henry sat very still, his eyes grown misty with guilt, the words in the rulebook swimming all but out of focus before his eyes . . . .

He suddenly sat up with a start. In another moment, without forewarning either to Katie or Charlie, he leaped from the car and began racing through the parking lot towards the press tent.

29

For nearly three hours – all through the televised programming of the United States Open – the golf-course back home at Rolling Hills Country Club, more than a thousand miles away, had never been so deserted. Nor had the men's grill been so overcrowded. The reason, of course, was that one of the club's members – now their most illustrious – was leading the most honoured golf tournament in the world, which was still slated for another ten minutes' of television coverage. Each time another twosome finished their third round of play, still unable to improve on Henry Summerfill's earlier-posted score, whoops of glee would ring out in the Rolling Hills clubhouse. A missed putt or an ill-directed tee-shot by one of the tournament favourites proved to be cause for downright elation among the membership. Now, Colin Montgomerie and Tom Lehman, the final twosome, were teeing off on the eighteenth hole. But neither had a chance to overtake amateur Henry Summerfill who, an hour earlier, had burst upon the golfing world like a comet. And no one was more confounded – or more elated – than that particular amateur's long-time golfing partner and enemy, Alex Wulf.

'I wonder if he can possibly sustain it for one more day,' speculated Dwight Lyon, who then shrugged his shoulders and sighed. 'He'll probably never play with us again, Alex. You know how guys get when fame strikes.' Dwight shook his head in disbelief. 'This has got to be the damnedest miracle in the history of golf.'

'In the history of *golf?*' challenged Alex Wulf. 'Hell, it's the greatest miracle in the history of the *world!*'

The crowded grill room quickly fell silent when Dick Enberg appeared on the TV screen, his countenance serious, his voice shifting gears into that tone announcers so capably reserve for only the most significant of pronouncements.

'Ladies and gentlemen,' he began. 'We of NBC have been told to stand by for something radically unusual about to take place. It is our understanding that amateur Henry Summerfill, who is leading this tournament, has hastily summoned all members of the USGA rules committee into the press tent where he is about to make a public announcement. Let's see if we can find out more about what to expect from our informed colleague Johnny Miller, who is there on the spot.'

'Thank you, Jim,' said Miller with solemn intensity. 'Sorry, but no one here has any better idea than you as to the nature of what Sommerfill is about to say. But we won't have to wonder much longer – Summerfill is now stepping up to a battery of microphones . . . .'

A thousand miles away at the Rolling Hills Country Club as well as in living-rooms and taverns and clubhouses and barber-shops throughout the country, 40 million curious viewers leaned nearer their television sets. And perhaps the two persons poised most delicately on the brink of suspense were Katie Summerfill and Charlie Bottomley who, having been denied entrance into the press tent, were now huddled along with more than a thousand alerted spectators in front of one of the mammoth screens on the terrace of the Spruce

Valley Clubhouse.

'I think maybe his brain his snapped,' Katie shivered as she spoke. 'The strain has just been too much for him. I think I know what he's going to say and – oh, Charlie, it's just awful!'

'Maybe he's physically ill and has become delirious,' offered Charlie. 'Golly, when he retrieved his ball from between my – my – you-knows, his fingers were groping so wildly I could hardly believe it.'

'Shhh! He's about to speak.'

Henry Summerfill gazed unflinchingly at the line-up of blue-blazered gentlemen facing him.

'Officials of the United States Golf Association,' he began in a surprisingly steady voice, 'ladies and gentlemen of the press and my fellow golfers everywhere. I stand here before you humbly and ashamed, for I am a man suffering under a burden of guilt . . . .'

When Henry paused, a world of television viewers paused with him, their hearts in their throats, waiting with awful anticipation for the confessional to follow.

'Golf is too great a game, too precious a pursuit, too proud a pastime to spoil with violations of its rules or its principles . . . . I do not ask that I be absolved from the wrongdoing I am about to confess. I only ask that you believe me when I say that my golfing crime was not one of malicious intent . . . .'

Katie Summerfill hung her tearful head.

Alex Wulf said, 'What in Chrissake is he talking about?'

The line-up of USGA officials forgot to puff on their pipes altogether.

Henry cleared his throat and launched into the guts of his announcement.

30

Headed for Rome, 40,000 feet above the Atlantic, Father Patrick O'Shane rested the *New York Times* on his portly priestly lap, then closed his eyes the more profoundly to meditate on the unusual front page editorial he had just read for the third time. When he opened his eyes again he gazed out past the airliner's wingtip towards Heaven, nodding a special thank you to the Lord for having influenced the editors of *The Times* to pay such prominent tribute to that inspirational, human-interest event of yesterday afternoon. The pink-cheeked priest smiled with satisfaction. Yes, just when he had concluded that all of mankind was racing towards Hell, God had seen to it that Father O'Shane's faith in his fellow man had not only been restored but buoyed to the point where he could hardly wait to deliver a rousing sermon based on the newspaper editorial. But he couldn't launch into an oration without an audience of at least one. His likeliest candidate, of course, was the gentleman with the black eye who occupied the aisle seat next to him. When the priest had first seated himself after boarding the plane late, the man, obviously embarrassed, had quickly slipped a book he was reading into his briefcase. It was only by chance that the observant father had glimpsed the title, *The Joy of Sex*, before it disappeared from view. And in these intervening two hours since leaving New York the man had seemed to doze continuously ... well, almost continuously. Father O'Shane, student of nature that he was, had noted that whenever a shapely flight attendant strolled by, the gentleman, as if having been granted psychic powers, would ease open one eye just long enough to feast on the splendour of the passing scene. The good father found it to be of considerable academic interest that while he and his travelling companion both admired the charms with which the Lord, in his generosity, had blessed these vibrant young women, Father O'Shane found himself stirred by their resulting shape and motion as they walked towards the front of the plane while his companion seemed more appreciative of their feminine charms as they headed back towards them. But despite that slight variance in the nature of their aesthetic tastes, Father O'Shane sensed that this man beside him would thrill with equal accord to the newspaper editorial which dealt with a different subject altogether. And the next time the gentleman fluttered open an eyelid, the alert father was ready.

'I say, my good fellow,' he began, 'what takes you to Europe, business or pleasure?'

The man smiled in acknowledgement. 'My dear sweet wife has been touring Europe with friends,' he said, 'and now I'm going to meet her.'

After a brief exchange of pleasantries, the priest's eyes lit up like two pale blue incandescent bulbs as he began focusing upon the glorious news he was so anxious to share .... 'By any chance, sir, do you follow golf tournaments?'

His neighbour looked back at him oddly, almost suspiciously. So much so, in fact, that Father O'Shane felt impelled to clarify his reason for having asked. He picked up the folded newspaper from his lap, opened it to the front page

187

and pointed a chubby ecclesiastic finger towards the featured editorial.

'I don't know whether you've read this or not,' enthused Father O'Shane, 'but it looks like America at last has a new national hero. Yes,' he went on, raising his voice a bit to attract the attention of others around him, 'the troops of our Lord have begun their counter-attack. And right now it's being led by a man who had it all in his grasp. He could have become the idol of millions, the rage of our age, a legend in his own—'

The good father was interrupted by a raspy voice a few rows to the rear.

'What the hell did the guy do? Find the Holy Grail?'

Father O'Shane frowned. 'I'm referring to a man who, through a newly-discovered gift of superlative golfing skill, propelled himself to heights of glory few have ever dreamed of attaining. Then quite by accident he discovered he had unwittingly violated one of the United States Golf Association's archaic rules. Despite the fact that no one would have even suspected his infringement of that regulation, he immediately chose to admit his guilt to the world, stripping himself of the robes of glory that already had begun mantling his shoulders . . . .'

'Don't tell us he shot his caddy,' someone shouted from the smoking section.

Father O'Shane paid the man no heed – he was too busy increasing the pitch and volume of his voice to include in his audience almost all of his fellow passengers. And while he had no intention of passing the plate either to raise funds for his parish or to underwrite a night of *la dolce vita* while in Rome, he did not intend to let his captive congregation off the hook without first exposing them to the finest sermon ever delivered aboard a TWA jumbo jet.

'But you still haven't told us what the man did.' Several

voices began to express impatience.

Much as the good father did not like others to dictate the orderly sequence of his pronouncements, he concluded it was wisest now to vindicate his general pontificating with factual specifics.

'The man's name,' he intoned, 'is Henry D. Summerfill the Third. He stood unflinchingly before the officials of that golfing organization and said, quote: *I have violated sub-section (1) of section four of Appendix IV of the Rules of Amateur Status. In short, gentlemen, as winner last month of the member-guest tournament, known as the Roundup at my local Rolling Hills Country Club, I was awarded a hand-sewn genuine Italian leather golf bag valued at five hundred and twenty dollars. The USGA rule in question states an amateur golfer may not accept either cash or merchandise exceeding five hundred dollars. Because of my acceptance of that prize, I falsely, though innocently, listed myself as an amateur on the official entry application of this great tournament so rich in the tradition of decency and fair play; I therefore disqualify myself from further play in this United States Open.'*

'Jesus, Father,' cried a man from business class. 'Oh, I'm sorry – I mean, golly, Father, everybody bets at golf. Guys win money or prizes all the time worth more than a puny five hundred bucks. That Summerfield guy must be off his rocker.'

'He is most certainly *not* off his rocker,' Father O'Shane countered. 'It's this crazy world that's off its rocker. If Summerfill's act of moral heroism doesn't make America sit up and take notice – if it doesn't make America cringe for the shallowness of its values – if it doesn't make America weep for its falsehoods and blush for its hypocrisies, then nothing ever will . . . .' Father O'Shane caught his breath when a buxom flight attendant cast him an over-the-shoulder smile as her mobile anatomy moved towards the front of the plane. But from years of having suffered through similar distractions, his voice only grew more sanctimonious. 'Despite so many evidences of our nation's sins and degradations we tend to forget – except when someone like Henry Summerfill steps forward – that there are still decent and gallant men and women among us – people of strong quiet devotion, of abiding faith, of uncompromising truth.'

By now it seemed to the good father that the entire planeload of passengers had turned their eyes and ears in his direction. He only hoped that if the crew from the cockpit had joined the throng, they had taken the precaution of putting the plane on automatic pilot. He smiled at his airborne brethren, then continued:

'Ah, but the noblest act of all followed shortly upon the heels of a hastily-summoned conference of the ruling officials at the tournament. Those gentlemen, realizing the inroads of inflation since the rule was made, unanimously voted to waive it, thus offering Henry Summerfill the right to rescind his self-disqualification.' The good father paused to intensify the dramatic impact of his next words . . . . 'And what did our heroic amateur have to say to those wishy-washy officials? He said, "In the game of golf as in the game of life, we must abide by the rules, or soon there will be no golf or life left to enjoy".'

Father O'Shane lifted his eyes and joined his fingertips beneath his chin . . . .

'Henry Summerfill, wherever you are, you have elevated all of our spirits to a higher, purer realm.'

Except for the faint far-away hum of the jet engines, the interior of the plane remained thoughtfully hushed, all eyes focused on the priest's benevolent face, all ears attuned to receive the blessings of his anticipated *amen*.

As he scanned the faces of his newly adopted flock, he was pleased to observe how effectively he had touched the gentleman beside him who was now wiping a tear from his blackened eye. But even as he did so, Father O'Shane could have sworn he detected a gleam springing up behind the tear – a gleam that perhaps was generated by the harmonious movement of the stewardess returning their way. In deference to his neighbour's momentary preoccupation, the considerate father waited until the young lady had passed by. He turned then with a final furtive gaze of his own before closing his eyes and dreamily chanting 'Amen.'

With his sermon concluded, he could not help but regret that he had no tape of his message to play back to himself prior to their scheduled arrival in Rome, especially seeing that his companion was dozing again. And yet, the more Father O'Shane studied the man's face, the more his neighbour's expression seemed to change. For one moment Father O'Shane thought he detected a look of pride. But what could this rather plain-looking mortal have done to feel proud of? Even as the good father speculated on that, the corners of the fellow's mouth seemed to hint at amusement. But why would this chap feel amused after just having been exposed to such a profound and solemn sermon? With growing puzzlement, Father O'Shane searched the face more closely to discern yet another change in expression. Yes, there was still pride, still amusement. But now, perhaps because the plane had climbed even nearer Heaven, the countenance of his fellow traveller was filled to overflowing with an expression of absolute and perfect peace.